The Critical Case

Sir Patrick Bijou

PRELUDE

The Critical Case is about the disappearance of a patient from a hospital in a horrifying and thrilling mystery drama. There is a picture of the man in the file, Argan Gregore. A convict from the Eastern Prison suffered a heart attack and was carried there urgently. He stayed at the hospital for two days and vanished without a trace. The obvious assumption would be that he escaped, but there was no sign of him ever leaving the hospital. The hospital is anxious about closing the matter as it will invariably damage its reputation.

An exciting and lesson-learning-based novel on what happened, the many twists that have occurred, and the unexpected ending makes a thrilling and nerve-clenching familiar plot that develops into an enthralling read.

ABOUT THE AUTHOR

Sir Patrick Bijou lives and writes from the United Kingdom and is the author of several books on finance and fiction. He is known for his extraordinary skills in settling and negotiating peace settlements and international law and is a prodigious legal and political adviser. His diverse writing ability has been influenced by many experiences, making him the success he is today.

Sir Patrick has written many books and articles about the liberation of people, highlighting the issues of those whom the literary world of creative writing has not enlightened. His expedition into content writing has made him a remarkably inspired author and professional communicator.

He has written over 32 non-fictional and fictional books spanning different genres.

Finding his Books.

To find out more about Sir Patrick, visit his website.

www.sirpatrickbijou.com
www.bijouebook.com

People trust me with their pets. They shouldn't.

That's what I thought as I stared at the empty leash in my hand. I rested my tired legs as I sat on a nearby bench. I couldn't return an empty leash to Mrs. Lashfield, my neighbor. She trusted me with her extremely dear dog, Flame, a gigantic yet adorable husky. Who had somehow managed to vanish into thin air?

My search across the park and all neighboring streets proved futile. I tried asking passersby if they had seen Flame, but they all shook heads and hurried off to work. It was a normal busy Monday morning, after all. Even shouting out her name didn't help. It only made me embarrassed because of the stares I was attracted to.

I released a deep sigh and tried not to freak out. I stood up, did some stretching, and got ready for search part two. As I started marching towards yet another street, my ringtone blasting out of my pockets made me stop. Praying it was not Mrs. Lashfield, I released a sigh of relief as I saw the name Attorney Kim flashing brightly on my mobile. I took the call.

"Be at the office in 30 minutes."

Good morning to you, too, Boss.

30 minutes, Haelyn.

"Sir, you may have failed to remember, but today is my day off-"

"I know. And I don't care. Be here in 30 minutes."

I scrunched up my nose in irritation. I started walking again, dragging an empty leash behind me. "But again, sir, I have a pressing matter right now that I need to handle."

An annoyed gruntle was heard from the other end. "Handle it first, or drag your issue to the office and handle it later. I don't care. Your job is the more urgent matter here." And he cut the call.

I put my phone back in my pocket and was about to cross the street and continue my search when I finally noticed her. There was that big bundle of a husky, across the street, under a tree. Taking a dump.

Relieved, I crossed the street and approached Flame, who noticed me and acted as if she didn't run away, making me spend an hour searching for her. She lifted her head, sticking her tongue out, and wagging her tail at me. Yes, that definitely didn't bring a smile to my face.

As she finished her toilet matters, I quickly put the leash on her again. Seeing that I was twenty minutes from the office, I decided to do some more different walks, this time my eyes strongly fixed on Flame and my hands having a stronghold onto the leash.

You will not get away again, buddy.

I arrived at the Harrington law firm soon enough, entering the steel grey building. Flame sauntered in front with confidence that she could pass as a worker here. Flame's barking quickly grabbed the attention of all the employees as I headed toward Attorney Kim's office on the third floor. Some were already stepping forward, reaching out to pet her. Flame, attention-loving as she was, wagged her tail eagerly.

"Not now, people," I said as I dragged Flame along, careful not to bump into the desks stacked with papers and files. Reaching at the far left end of the corridor where Attorney Kim's office was situated, I knocked on the door twice and waited. I heard his faint voice from inside telling me to enter. I opened the door and let Flame enter first as I followed behind. "Come, sit dow-" he started before he stopped at the sight of the enormous dog who went straight up next to him and sat down, staring at him. "What is this?

You know animals aren't allowed here, right?" he asked in a clipped tone while narrowing his eyes at Flame.

"But sir, you told me to either handle my issue first, which I couldn't or drag my issue to the office, which I did."

Attorney Kim huffed with annoyance and ignored me. Instead, he reached into one of his drawers and took out a file. My eyes followed the file as I reached for one of the chairs and sat down. Then he reached out for another file and handed it over to me.

"This is a case we need to prepare on. It's actually a case from a few days ago. No one took the case as they supposedly already had priorities. Mr. Lawson gave it to me today, but I am already handling that murder case from last week. The file I gave you is a copy. Prepare the details and report well. I'll attend to it as soon as I finish the current case."

"The complaint is against the Wellsworth Hospital? Isn't that one of those important hospitals uptown?" I asked while rummaging through the pages, trying to process all data in my mind.

"Yes. The case is about the disappearance of one of the patients. There is a picture of the man in the file. Argan Gregore. A convict from the Eastern Prison. He suffered from a heart attack and was carried there urgently. He stayed there for two days, and then no trace of him after. The obvious assumption would be that he escaped. But there was no sign of him leaving the hospital. And the hospital is hell-bent on closing the matter because it will damage their reputation."

"Who was the one who filed the complaint then? The prison?" "No, they couldn't care less. The prisoner's brother filed a case against the hospital, so we can't keep procrastinating on it for so long. Anyway, that's all I can tell you right now. Go through it and make sure we are able to close the case soon," he said as he motioned me to get out now. I stood up, with the file in one hand and the leash in another, and headed out.

After buying a drink from the office's vending machine, I headed to my table.

While most attorneys and lawyers had their own office, the legal secretaries and paralegals were all packed on the third floor.

I sat down with a thud on my chair and dumped the file on my table. I let Flame walk around as my colleagues showered her with attention, love, and, most importantly, treats. As for me, the tiring hours of walking finally caught up on me.

"Why are you here today?"

"I love my job too much, so I don't want a day off. I want to work, duh." I said sarcastically to my best friend, Eliyah, whose table was right across me.

Eliyah McKenry. I've known her for a decade, since high school. I never expected us to end up working at the same place since she moved to Lancashire for university and stayed to work there itself. While I joined the Harrington law firm three years ago, she joined only a year ago when she moved back to London due to my great efforts and skills at convincing her.

"Oh, did Attorney Kim pull an 'urgent case' again on you?" She laughed.

I stared blankly at her and handed her the file. She glanced through the pages as I filled her in on the details.

"Well, see the good side. You'll be on your own. He won't be poking his nose into the case with his constant commentaries. He's still busy with the murder case, and Eric is stuck with him."

I nodded in agreement. Though Attorney Kim tolerates my foolishness most of the time, he is very strict and thorough on his cases which is very scary when assisting him in his work.

"Anyway, what's up? You said you wanted to give me some good news yesterday," I said while leaning back in my chair, closing my eyes momentarily.

"Oh yes! Exciting news!" Eli beamed. I would guess she probably heard another insignificant gossip here and there, as she always fills me in with gossip I don't care about.

"Really!" I said, trying to sound excited. But it only came out as nonchalant. Eli glared at me and then smiled again.

"I assure you, you'll be very happy," she insisted.

By all means, go on.

Castiel Alpens is back.

"What?" I asked in a gentle tone as I sat up straight. Eli crossed her arms and smiled smugly at me.

I scoffed and asked, "Where did you get that from?" "One of the high school group chats."

"Those group chats are still alive?" I wondered. Usually, those group chats disappear mere months after school despite promises to keep in touch.

"I created one again after the last reunion, which someone didn't attend, obviously," Eli said as she rolled her eyes at me.

"Anyway," she continued back on the topic, "Castiel returned after two years in Turkey. Brian filled us in."

Pfft, this was in no way good news for me. There was no reason for it to be. Castiel Alpen was one of my high school classmates. Leave us alone for a second, and we'd be at each other's throats.

We would never miss an opportunity to insult each other while still being able to be civil and all smiles. Castiel was like a balloon of ego, one that I really wished to prick with a needle. He was also a very competitive guy, probably to be able to boost his confidence even more. I wasn't one to put up with his ego, so we clashed a lot. We always competed to be number one in our school—me doing so only to annoy him.

Last time, I heard he went to Turkey to join the International Operation Forces training program. The IOF organization has gained recognition worldwide for being one of the world's best law enforcement. Its headquarters are splattered all over the globe in several countries.

The training Castiel had was a six months duration of Special Agent training. I envied that; the idea of being a Special Agent seemed so cool for a small paralegal like me. If I ever got a chance to join them, I'd go running at them. The only issue was that the training was tough, and only a few were selected.

"Hey ho, are you thinking of him?" I heard a nagging voice break my bubble of thoughts.

I sighed, stood up, and grabbed my file. "I think I'll start with the hospital first," I pondered while again flipping the pages.

"Don't you think we should meet again since he's back? You haven't seen him in six years, right?"

Eli mused over the idea with a gleam in her eyes.

"We don't want to start World War III, Eli. And I gotta go. I'm a busy working woman."

"Flame! Time to go!" I yelled for the dog to come back from wherever she was. I decided to bring her back to her owner, leaving out some useless details like I almost lost her dog.

After lunch, I headed to Wellsworth Hospital. I already had some questions ready. The sooner I carried out the research, the better.

I headed to the reception, showed my work ID, and asked if I could talk to Dr. Martinez, the one responsible for the disappeared patient. The receptionist called someone, talked a bit, and informed me that Dr. Martinez was in the middle of an operation. I decided to wait for him to finish the operation and asked the receptionist to inform me when he was finished.

I checked my watch again. I kept shaking my legs as I emptied my eighth cup of coffee. I've been waiting for Dr. Martinez for four hours now. Still no sign of him. I inquired at the reception again, and they said some operations could take hours.

I sat in a secluded area to not interrupt the constant movement of patients and doctors. I glanced around, bored. All I wanted to do was to break into the operation room and drag that doctor away from his operation. Maybe I should talk to the administrative team first.

Just as my eyes wandered around, I caught sight of the receptionist walking towards one of the doctors. I heard her mutter the doctor's name. I quickly stood up, ignoring the feel of pins and needles in my legs, and rushed towards the doctor.

He, too, seemed to be in a rush. Pshh, it's like he's trying to run away from me.

I interrupted both the doctor and the receptionist. "Dr. Martinez?" I confirmed. His exasperated look changed to a professionally composed one. "May I help you?"

"I assume you've already been informed of my presence and the reason why. I need to interview-"

"I'm sorry, but I guess that's something that will take time. I have a very tight schedule, and I don't have time now," Dr. Martinez blurted as he tried to brush past me and walk away. I stopped him.

"This is a pressing case for you as well. I need only five minutes. This concerns a complaint against this hospital. And before the administrative team, I wished to ask a few things of you."

He seemed to have lost his calm composure. "This case won't bring down our hospital if you could let the police handle the investigation and also reserve your questions for them. Such constant visits are disrupting the hospital schedules!"

"Sir, this is MY case, and I'm legally allowed to interview you on the matter-" I started before he, again, interjected.

"Then try getting an appointment." That's all he said before he practically ran out of the hospital.

I huffed and slowly followed out as well. So rude. People look down upon us as assistants. I'm only doing my job. As I walked out and into my car, I glanced up and saw that it's almost dark. Damn it! I groaned. A day off was totally wasted.

I opened the file and searched through it. I reached the contact number and called it.

"Hello?" A deep voice resounded from the phone. "Hello. Argus Gregore? I'm Haelyn Carter, responsible for the case of your brother. Can we meet tomorrow?"

I was at the Starlight Cafe, munching on my chocolate muffin. Seated near the window, I stared outside blankly while waiting for Argus Gregore's arrival.

A cough from behind disrupted my daydream, and I turned around to see a young man, maybe around my age, with dark brown curly hair and green eyes. He wore a casual shirt and ripped jeans. His eyes surveyed me questioningly.

"Argus Gregore?" I confirmed. He nodded. I stood up, shook his hand, and motioned him to sit down next to me.

"You want to order something before we start?" I asked.

"It's okay, I already ordered when I entered. And I'm sorry I arrived a bit late. I had to ask my friend to pick me up as my car is not in a good state right now," he said with an apologetic smile.

"No problem. At least you didn't refuse to see me, unlike some people," I muttered with a scowl as I thought of yesterday.

Argus let out a bitter laugh and said, "Let me guess, Dr. Martinez?"

I nodded and took out my phone, and put on the recorder. "I'm guessing you've met him already."

"I met him on the second day of my brother's disappearance, and he said he could not waste his time enlightening everyone on the case. He told me to contact the police for any questions I had and not to bother him. He seems too busy for anything apart from his job," he said with a scoff.

"Did you meet with your brother prior to his disappearance?"

"Uhm, no," he coughed out and took a sip of water before he continued. "I visited him a few times in jail some years ago. But then, I went to Italy and decided to live there. Since then, I have never met up with him again. Though I intended to see him again when he was out."

"According to you, do you really think your brother escaped? His sentence was to end in a month anyway."

"There could still be a possibility," he confessed.

After some more questions, I sighed. Argus Gregore was of no help in all seriousness. He knew nothing about the subject since he had been in Italy for a while. We just kept circling on the same point.

"What is your age?" I asked after a pause.

Argus was startled by the out-of-subject question but still replied, "Twenty-two." Oh, he's young.

"You work?"

"I'm working some part-time jobs back in Italy," he said as he looked at me puzzled, probably wondering where I was going with these questions.

"You went to university?"

"No, I don't have enough money. Why are you asking all these questions? I thought we were supposed to talk about my brother," he said, now being defensive as I probed deeper.

"Chill. It's all connected. From what I got from the information I have, you were under the guardianship of your brother since the age of thirteen, after your parents' death. Your brother was twenty back then. Five years after, he was arrested on the charge of assault on his then-girlfriend. Anyway, my question is, how close are you two?" I asked in a curious tone.

After a few minutes of silence, Argus pondered the question a bit and replied, "We are just as close as any other brothers. He was busy most of the time, though, having to earn to support us both."

"Did you intend on reuniting with him after he finished his sentence?" "Yes," Argus started hesitantly, "but I would return to Italy, where I'm currently residing. My brother would have more likely remained here."

Ending the recording, I stood up as he followed along. "This is it for now. If you have anything important to say, you can contact me," I said to him as he nodded. We shook hands, and both of us left. Well, me much later. I wanted more cake.

After leaving the cafe, I went straight to the law firm. I checked in Attorney Kim's office, but he wasn't there. I looked around to see whose help I could ask. Even Eliyah was not here today. She must have accompanied Mr. Cortez in the trial.

Just then, I saw Mr. Lawson enter the building. The Managing Partner of the firm. The right person. I approached him with a bright smile. "Good morning, Mr. Lawson."

"Good morning, Haelyn. How are you today?" He asked warmly.

"Very fine, except for one small trouble that you could be able to help me with, if I may ask, that is," I asked, chuckling nervously.

He laughed and motioned me to follow him to his office. I released a breath of relief and followed.

"Tell me, what do you need?" Mr. Lawson asked after settling in his chair.

"Just one phone call, sir. I've had trouble getting an appointment with Dr. Martinez from Wellsworth Hospital. I wanted to talk to him before going to the hospital's legal department. Since you are well known around here, I hoped you could arrange for me to get some minutes with him," I pleaded.

I knew that doctor wouldn't concede to me alone. If someone with more power and connections did so, then he wouldn't have much choice, I thought smugly. "So, only one call?" Mr. Lawson confirmed. I nodded eagerly with my hands clasped together in a pleading manner.

"Give me a minute," he said. I waited as he called some people and spoke a bit. After a few minutes, he ended the call. "Well, Dr. Martinez seems like a tough person to convince. He agreed to spare you five minutes only in an hour. Is that okay with you?"

I mentally rolled my eyes. Dr. Martinez really thought his time was golden. I'll show him. He won't get rid of me easily.

Putting on a smile, I replied, "Works for me, Sir. Thank you very much. Have a nice day."

I arrived fifteen minutes early at the hospital. I got my papers and questions ready. I cracked my knuckles, sat down, and waited.

If someone saw my face, they'd think I was getting ready for a fire rap battle. Five minutes. That's all I had. And that's all I needed to defeat him. I grinned evilly.

A man with a cast around his arm sat across me, probably a patient. He was giving me a weird stare. I guess it was because I was grinning to myself. What can I say, though? As someone who's in the legal field, I was so used to engaging in mental arguments, which was reflected in my real expressions.

Finally, I saw Dr. Martinez pass by, thoroughly ignoring me as he entered his office. Anyway, I had to make my presence known. I walked up to his door and knocked. I heard him say come in.

I opened the door, and before he could say anything, I grinned widely and said, "Hello again, Sir. I tried to make an appointment, and I got one. Will I have my five minutes?"

He stared at me for seconds and said, "Only five minutes. Let's get this over with. What are your questions?"

Well, look at his guts. He did not even ask me to take a seat. You onion-eyed barnacle!

"I want to know some things about Argan Gregore. You operated on him. Was he alright after? When was the last time anybody saw him? Do you believe he escaped? Isn't their security in each corner here? Wasn't his room guarded as well since he was a prisoner?" I looked at him expectantly. I hoped he would not stall with his answers because I had only five minutes.

"He was stable but unconscious. I checked on him three hours before his disappearance. Since he was unconscious, there was no reason to have guards here. He probably escaped, though, if he regained consciousness," he remarked.

"Does the hospital have cameras installed in patients' rooms?"

"No hospitals do this due to patient privacy."

"Do you have camera surveillance records of the entrance and exit, then?"

"We already checked."

"Well, can I recheck?"

"You need special permission to get your hands on that," he grumbled snobbishly.3 I rolled my eyes at him. "Well, I will ask the hospital's legal team for it then," I said calmly, with a nonchalant shrug.

"Your time is up." Dr. Martinez said suddenly. What? So quick! I couldn't lose the battle!

"Don't you care that your hospital let loose a prisoner who is potentially dangerous?" I said as I got up slowly. Maybe I could finish the interview before I reached the door.

"I did my job as a doctor by saving him, Miss Carter. Guarding him is not my responsibility, nor is the protection of the public. I believe the police are doing their job searching for him. And can you please stop this slow moonwalk of yours and get out quickly? I don't have all the time in the world for you."

"If you get additional information, you can contact-"

"No."

I let out an irritated scream mentally and got out. I closed the door a bit loudly for effect.

No one was really helping me with my report-making. Since the police were already investigating about it, should I stop pretending to be a detective and let them do their job while I waited?

As I sat at my desk with papers scattered, I thought about what to do as I had my head pressed by both hands on the table. Ideas, ideas, where are you?

I slammed my head on my desk. The police were so bad at their job! It's been a week already. How come they haven't found Argan Gregore yet?

But then, here I was, clueless about what to do. I sucked at my job as well.

Then the idea came. I snapped my fingers. Contacts.

In the legal field, contacts mattered a lot. Ronan Carter was one of my best close contacts. Working in the police and as a detective for thirty years, he established an honorable reputation for himself across the country and abroad. His contacts could be of some help to me, I hoped. I took my phone and called.

"Dad? I need help!" I asked as soon as the call connected.

"Wow, no, hello, no, how are you, nothing? I feel so used," I heard a teasing voice on the other end.

"Hello! How are you? I bet you're fine. I need help," I replied with a grin.

"Yes. I am fine. How could I be of any help? I'm at work right now."

"Perfect. Can you contact Officer Philip and tell him to call Mr. Flynn, and for Mr. Flynn to call Mr. Duncan, and for Mr. Duncan to contact the Eastern police station and relay the message that I request the past week's CCTV footage of the Wellsworth Hospital?"

There was a long pause, and I heard a big sigh.

"Am I your slave?"

"It's a favor. I'll repay you whenever you want. Does a bag of brownies work for now?"

Okay, deal.

"Thanks! Talk to you later. Love you, bye."

I headed to the nearest police station where Mr. Duncan worked. Because of their search for the supposedly escaped prisoner, they got hold of the CCTV footage to check the records from the day

Argan 'escaped.' And because the CCTV footage was apparently too precious, they asked me to come to check instead of them sending it.

I entered Mr. Duncan's office. He was occupied with some files and, without looking up, gestured for me to sit down. "Hello, sir. You got the video footage?" "Here, they are on this laptop," he said, pushing a laptop towards me, "You can check them yourself, but you are not allowed to transfer them to any of your electronic devices."

So I started viewing the CCTV footage. I sat there for almost two hours, skipping some parts and trying to memorize as much as possible. The entrance area was too obvious for someone to escape, and as I thought, there was no sign of anyone suspicious walking out.

I checked the exit area's records. No one seemed suspicious enough. Doctors were leaving, doctors arriving, some probably doctor's assistants or male nurses transferring a dead body onto an ambulance-

Wait, wait! Wouldn't that be an astounding escaping idea?

But then, the medical team would have noticed if he escaped after. I was overthinking unless they took him for a ghost.

In this world where everything is possible, we should not let any suppositions slip away. When Mr. Duncan wasn't looking, I snapped pictures of the scene. It'll suffice. Then I checked the rest of the footage for any other similar possibilities.

I arrived at the hospital for the third time. I was becoming very familiar with it. And right now, of course, paying a visit to Dr. Martinez was out of the question. I didn't want to risk getting kicked out by security guards.

I walked inside and then just stood in the middle. I liked wandering into places without a plan.

I walked past the reception area, getting an 'again?' look from the receptionist. I smiled and walked past her. I continued walking, looking around about who to ask and what to ask. I saw a nurse walk out of a patient's room holding a writing board.

"Excuse me!" I called out as she was passing by me. She looked up in my direction, surprised and wondering who I was.

"Hello, I'm Haelyn Carter," I said, showing my work ID, "I am currently making a report on the last week's disappearance issue. Can I ask you a question? It won't take time." "Sure. If it helps," she said, offering a smile. Thank God, not all people were Martinez-style here.

I took out my phone and showed her the photos I had taken from the CCTV footage.

"Do you know these people? Are they employees of the hospital? Doctors, assistants, or nurses?"

The nurse took my phone and zoomed in to see well as she scrunched her nose in concentration. "I think I may have seen one of the men here, a male nurse. But the other, no. I never saw him. Still, I'm not sure because this seems a bit blurry."

"And can I get to see the records of patients who sign out of the hospital or those who passed away here?" "I don't have access to the records, and I don't think you'll be allowed to as well. But I would recommend you to ask the administration department and see if they can help," she said, offering to guide me there. When we arrived at the desk, I again introduced myself and showed my ID while the nurse left to continue with her work. I wished to see the papers and records besides the man to whom I was explaining my situation. I firmly refused to have a look at any of their data records, considering me being a petty paralegal, not that he mentioned that part, but at this point, I'm already used to it.

"But by any chance, were there any deceased patients taken out the day that prisoner escaped? I'm not asking for any name or other details, just a confirmation of yes or no," I asked the man, who was now on his computer.

"No, none that day," he confirmed after browsing the computer. I thanked him and left.

But my eyes didn't deceive me. I did see a dead body.

I had to make sure I saw it correctly or was mistaken. But if it wasn't a dead body, what could it be? A bag of potatoes?

I headed to the police station again the next day. I looked around, but there was no sign of Mr. Duncan. I asked one of the constables about his whereabouts and found out that he was away because of a nearby hit-and-run accident.

"I came here yesterday to check the CCTV footage of the Wellsworth Hospital, representing the Harrington law firm. Do you have the CCTV footage? Can I check something for a minute?" I requested.

The constable accepted and directed me toward one of their computers. I sat down and started going through it again. Soon, I became frustrated with the computer. I called the constable again.

"Is something wrong with the computer? Why are there so many glitches on it?"

The constable shook his head and sighed. "I went through the records many times and even checked the computer. Nothing is wrong. I confirmed with other police stations and the prison that received the CCTV footage. All of them got the camera footage and had glitches in them."

"The CCTV footage worked quite fine on Mr. Duncan's laptop," I remarked.

"Did you check everything? I'm sure there were some glitches, though he took them directly from the hospital. The people from the hospital themselves stated that there had been some problem with their CCTV cameras for some days, and they are being repaired now. It's useless checking the CCTV footage right now. The police are doing their best to look for the escaped prisoner," the constable explained and walked away.

I rubbed my temples into concentration. Mr. Duncan got the footage from the hospital, and it worked just fine. The camera footage the police stations received was handed over to them by the hospital.

What if the CCTV footage was tampered with by somebody before it was given to the police stations? I slammed my hands on the desk loudly and stood up so quickly that the chair screeched back. Yes, that's it!

Then I noticed the silence in the middle of my amazing temporary conclusion. Everyone stopped their work and looked at me. I could feel the judgment in their eyes.

I chuckled nervously and clapped my hands in the air. "Ahaha, it's just those flies. They are such pests." And I walked out quickly to avoid further embarrassment.

After lunch, I sat at my desk again, searching for inspiration as I analyzed the pictures I had taken.

"Has the burglary case finally been closed?" I asked Eliyah, who was busy typing something on her laptop. "Yup, I'm just finishing its report right now."

I sighed and looked back at my phone. Eliyah's eyes wandered to me for a second before she continued typing. "What's up with your case?" she inquired.

"Pfft, finally, you asked!" I exclaimed and started ranting off about my problems, difficulties, complaints, or whatever they could be called.

"I am at a dead end," I finished. By then, Eliyah had already stopped typing, closed her laptop, and was listening to me.

"Give me your phone," she demanded. I handed it over to her as she looked at the pictures as well.

"Did you search the ambulance in the picture by its license plate?"

"I did. I looked around for it and asked some of the security guards. They said it was sent for repairs."

"Hmm, you could go check for it wherever it was sent to be repaired. Maybe you could get a little hint by asking around. Like who drove it there or when it was sent there, before the disappearance or after."

"Yes! I'd know then if it was the two men who were seen in the CCTV footage. Or I could get better CCTV footage if there is any surveillance camera at that auto repair shop."

I got up and took my bag and phone. "Thanks, Boo," I grinned as I rushed past her and ruffled her hair. I knew she hated that, but she didn't get the chance to yell as I ran past her.

I sat in my car and searched for all the auto repair shops nearby. There were three, so I decided to check each. The first one had no ambulance that was there for repair, so I moved on to the next.

I arrived at Fix Auto West London after thirty minutes. I looked around to ask someone, but everyone seemed busy.

"Hey, lady! Do you need something?" I heard from beneath me as I jumped back, stunned. Someone slid out from under a car that was next to me.

He seemed to be in his forties. He had dust, and black dirt smeared all over his clothes.

Are you the owner of this place?

"Yes, I am. Do you need help with your car or something?" he asked, gesturing to my park outside.

I shook my head. "No, I came here to check something. By any chance, was an ambulance from the Wellsworth Hospital sent here for repair?"

"Yes, there it is," he said, gesturing to one at the far end of the place. I ran to it and pulled out my phone. I looked at the license plate. LA13SBR. Yes, that's it! The owner followed me in a perplexed manner. "I wonder how this ambulance could interest you."

"Oh," I took out my work ID and showed him, "I am making a report on a case related to the Wellsworth Hospital. And my curiosity led me here. And this ambulance here may be of big importance to me," I said as I patted it and laughed.

"I still don't understand...," the owner trailed off.

"First of all, I want to know when did this ambulance arrive here?"

"Last week. 20th May, I think."

"How many people were there in the ambulance?"

Only the driver.

Wait. But it doesn't click. There are supposed to be two men. Or three. If the 'dead body' counts. Unless they got off earlier.

"Does your repair shop has a surveillance camera?" I asked, glancing around.

"No, but we have one outside," he said, pointing to one to the left, outside near the road.

"Perhaps, I could check them, please," I asked.

"Yes, sure," he said and smiled. He turned around and yelled, "Louis! Show the lady the camera footage of last week." A young guy popped out from under a car and walked over to me.

"That's my son," the owner said, patting his back, "he'll show you whatever you need. I need to get going."

"Thank you," I said gratefully.

"Anytime," he smiled and left.

The boy, Louis, guided me over to a compact office at the corner of the repair shop. He turned on the computer. "Only the records of last week?" he asked.

"I need only the records of the 20th May."

He stood up and gestured for me to sit down instead. I sat down and started going through the records.

"Are you searching for something specific? I could help," Louis offered.

"Yes, were you there that day? I need the CCTV footage at the time the ambulance arrived." "Yes. I'm not sure about the exact time, but it must have been around noon," he said after a thought.

I quickly searched through the camera footage around that time and finally saw it. But then, it just passed and entered inside. I got no glimpse of the driver. My fingers brushed through my hair in annoyance as I kept replaying it.

"Did you see the driver?" I turned to the boy while taking out my phone and showing him the picture. "Was it one of those men?"

"I can't tell. This picture is blurry, and the driver actually had a mask covering his face. Because of a cold or something," he said.

My eyes went back to the camera footage. I continued playing the records after the ambulance went in. Five minutes later, a black car appeared in the video. I stood straight with attention, my hands already reaching for my phone. The black car waited there for a while until a man came out of the repair shop and got into the car.

I took some pictures of the car. That's all I can get from here. I stood up and turned to the boy,

"Thank you, both you and your father. That is a lot of help." Then I walked back to my car.

I returned to the law firm and passed by the hospital. Should I check right now or later? Maybe it was better to do so now. It was already afternoon anyway.

I entered the hospital parking lot. There was a fifty percent chance the black car belonged to one of the hospital employees. I drove around the parking lot slowly, searching for the car. I checked all the black cars until I finally spotted the right one. Checking all details to be certain, I parked right across it and stared at it. All I can do right now is wait. I looked at my watch. 4 pm right now.

My wait lasted an hour or so. I had even been taking walks in between. Was it really worth wasting my time? Or would I be able to confirm my doubts? I knew I didn't have to do this. All I needed was a report. But fact-checking would harm no one, right?

As I took my fifth walk and approached my car, I saw the black car pulling out. And it left.

Wasting no time or thoughts, I rushed to my car, got in, fastened my seatbelt, started it, and followed after.

I started tailing the car and made sure I remained close behind. I allowed no car to get in between and interrupt my pursuit. I couldn't even get a good look at the driver. I kept my car right behind him for about fifteen minutes.

Then I started suspecting that he knew I was following him. I noticed how he kept glancing at his side mirror, and his doubts seemed to have increased when I followed him as he sped up into complicated roads here and there. Soon he stopped sideways, maybe to check if I was going to stop or go ahead.

I decided to pass by. I put my hair sideways to hide my face, but as I went ahead, I saw him take out his phone. Oh no! He took a picture of my car!

Taking out my phone, I called Eliyah. "Hey, I'm returning from the auto repair shop. But I need my motorbike. Can you get it to the front of the law firm for me right now?"

"Okay, why?"

"I'll explain after. Just get it to the front, quick!"

I took a left turn and went to the law firm. I saw Eliyah waiting for me, leaning against my black beauty, my bike, with the helmet in her hands. The bike was a gift from my Dad on my 18th birthday. I was crazier for a bike than a car back then. I bought the car only a few months ago.

I rushed out of the car and threw the car keys at Eliyah to catch.

"Take my car back to my apartment," I said as I got on my bike. "Oh, and your black hoodie looks nice. Let's swap!" I said, taking off my jacket and handing it to her. Though she was puzzled by my actions, she followed suit.

"What kind of shit are you getting yourself into?" she asked in a serious tone as she watched me put on her hoodie.

"Let's just say I'm playing catch the criminal game," I grinned and patted her shoulders, "Don't worry, I'll be safe."

"Oh, by the way, there is a gathering at Brian's apartment after dinner. Will you be there?"

"I might be there, a bit late, but still there," I said as I put on my helmet.

"Don't do anything stupid. And don't be late. Other friends will be there too. Especially Cas-"

"We'll see, Eli. For now, I'm in a hurry," I interrupted her.

And then, I took a turn and returned to the freeway. Seeing that the car was on the freeway all the time, I assumed he could be going out of town. By now, he may be a bit ahead of me while staying on the lookout for my car. Ha! Guess who's the smarter one!

I spent some minutes speeding past cars here and there until I got back on track behind the black car. The driver seemed more at ease now, with no doubt that the pursuer was behind him.

We got out of London and into Hertfordshire quite fast. I made sure this time to avoid any suspicions. Sometimes I took other routes to distract him. Or sometimes, I would stall behind and then catch up after.

As we continued, the vehicles decreased in number and the sky grew darker in color, and night crept in slowly. I no longer knew where I was going, but I had come too far to stop now. I could only continue following the car to avoid getting more lost than I am right now.

The roads the car took became narrower and bumpy. There was only him and I now. I stayed far behind, far enough for him not to see me. And soon, I was the one that couldn't see him at all. The road came to a dead end, or more like a mud path into a forest of some sort.

I stopped near a cabin, which I ensured was empty and abandoned. I hid my bike behind it so no one could get a glimpse of it.

I checked my phone. It was almost 7 pm now. I needed to hurry and leave. But before that, I need to search for a black car. I used my phone's flashlight to get around.

I followed the path in the woods, not paying attention to the mud sticking to my shoes. It was totally dark. And the air was chilly with the continuous breezes. I couldn't see anything except trees, trees, and most trees. There was no sign of the car, the man, or even any noise around. At some point, I gave up and leaned against a tree to rest. I was hungry. It had been eight hours since I ate lunch.

Then I heard a vibrating sound. I listened quietly. It seemed like the sound of a car! But no, it seemed a bit louder. I couldn't be sure. I jogged in the direction of the sound, sometimes falling and tripping against tree roots.

I finally found myself back on the road. A poorly paved one that is. I saw the light ahead. I turned off my flashlight so as not to arouse suspicion. I continued my way among the trees, trying to walk by feeling each tree with my hand.

The path became clearer as I approached the light.

The view became clearer and clearer. And just in front of me was the black car I followed, another black car, and a truck. I was sure it was the truck's noise that guided me here.

And all those vehicles were parked in front of an old building. Windows were missing almost everywhere. The building seemed like an old warehouse, with moss covering the outside. Just then, I saw three people opening the back of the truck and dragging out something long, wrapped in a large bag thrown over one of the man's shoulders.

This is definitely not a bag of potatoes! What am I getting myself into?

Now, what do I do? Enjoy the show? Though there was no good show from my audience seat.

I hid behind a tree in a daze for at least five minutes before regaining my composure. I shall enjoy the show from the first-row seat.

There was no one guarding the entrance and the surroundings. That means they were sure about their hiding, and no one would discover them. But guess who's here, lads!

I crept to the back of the warehouse. I was going to hide against the wall, but seeing the moss-covered walls with small insects crawling around, I refrained from touching it.

But from my position at the back, I couldn't see anything or hear anyone. This isn't going to work. I need to slip in without them noticing. I walked around, moving to the side of the building. The skittering of a few pebbles that I kicked echoed around, making me move to the moss-covered ground that helped to stifle the sound of my footsteps.

I marched to the left side of the building, where the light from inside seemed dim. The people inside were probably far from where I was standing. I looked up and spotted the window...or the lack thereof. There was no sign of any bits of window glass which meant I could easily slip in. This was gonna be my entrance.

Seeing that it was a bit high, I decided to jump and hold on fast then try to crawl in. I regretted it as fast as I fell back. The surrounding seemed a bit rusty, and I cut the palm of my hands as soon as I held onto it.

As I held on again, I tugged onto the hoodie's sleeves to cover my hands. Damn, the hoodie is getting dirty! Someone is going to be mad at me later. Ugh, never mind. I'll just buy her a new one.

With some effort, I threw one leg inside and balanced half of my body. I stayed still for a few seconds to ensure no one was nearby. Then I entered the room in a backward position. I steadied myself with my hands on the wall. Well, it seemed cleaner inside!

But the air seemed eerie.

I looked around, but it was totally dark. My hand reached out for my phone as I turned on my camera flashlight. The light helped me scan my surrounding a bit, which seemed empty. The door was kept slightly ajar.

I started to walk forward when my left foot met an obstacle. I stood back on my steps rigidly. The obstacle didn't feel hard enough to be an object. A smell hit me as I took a deep breath to calm myself. I pinched my nose and closed my eyes for a few seconds.

Sending a quick prayer to God, I directed my camera's light below on the floor. And all I saw was white. Something wrapped in white. Or someone.

I let out a silent gasp as I fell to the floor and hurried back into the corner of the room. I kept my trembling hand pressed over my mouth to prevent myself from making any sound. I stared, stared, and continued staring with wide eyes. I felt my heartbeats echoing around the almost empty room. It was not every day that I encountered a dead body. This was not in my job description!

Taking a deep breath, I flashed my light again on the body. Should I check it? No, no, I can't touch...that. I was supposed to be investigating on a supposedly escaped prisoner. Could this be him? Now I knew what that smell was. It was the putrid foul smell of the decomposing body. Whoever the person is, he must have been dead for a while.

My breaths quickened. I needed to get out of here. The smell started to be suffocating. As my hands reached towards the window to escape, I heard faint voices outside. I immediately retracted my hands. Maybe going out would be a bad idea for now.

I moved towards the door instead. The door's handle was rusty, so I pushed the door to open it further and peeked outside. No one in sight! I started to move out slowly. I turned off the light in case I'd get noticed by one of the men. The warehouse seemed very much abandoned. The smell of moss and dew was everywhere. Even the floor was slippery. In other parts of the building, I could hear droplets of water dripping. There were bits of metal, rusted and broken, lying around. My footsteps echoed on the empty floor as I walked.

I followed the source of light. And as I approached, I could hear the sound of their voices. I halted some meters away from the mysterious people and stood close to the moist wall. I again took out my phone and put it on the recording. I couldn't just leave empty-handed.

"The truck will pass by in a week. There is enough time to move it all."

"No need to be concerned with it. For now, you should return and keep away for a while."

"Yes, Doctor."

Doctor? Doctor who? What's a doctor doing here?

Despite trying to get a good look at them, the wall blocked the whole view, and I couldn't risk even a peek.

"And what about the bodies?"

Bodies? Bodies as in plural? Oh Lord, what did I stick my butt into?

"The usual waste disposal. Get rid of them without raising suspicions."

"We are already being suspected by some people."

"I told you, dumbasses, to be careful! You are not new to this. Who are these people?" "Some undercover agents have discovered our activities in the North. Many times, our plans had to be canceled. And here, there is that girl who keeps sticking her ass in our business with an investigation no one asked her to carry out."

Pshh, you don't mean me by any chance.

"Some Haelyn Carter. She even tried tailing my car today. She lost me midway, though."

Oh.

"The Boss won't be happy with more nails in our path. Keep your eyes on her. Don't let her get too close."

Close like what? Some meters away?

"And get rid of her if she does."

I instinctively took a step back. I think I heard enough. It's time to go. I tiptoed my way backward slowly.

Just then, I heard someone approaching in my direction. I quickly jumped into one of the rooms. Whoever the person is, he simply walked by without looking inside. But the men's voices were a bit louder. Were they leaving?

I tried to push the door quietly to remain unnoticed. CLINK!

I froze in place. Everywhere was still for a second. My head slowly moved downwards. The door's handle had fallen on the ground.

Idiot.

Idiot!

IDIOT!

I held my breath and waited. Silence. Complete silence.

"Julian. Claris. Check the building!" a voice suddenly boomed, echoing throughout the place. Then, I heard the rushing of footsteps. I was no longer calm. I looked around with agitation and saw the passage outside, where there used to be a window. I quickly leaped and jumped over, falling outside.

By reflex, I immediately covered my head with the hoodie. I heard some people opening the front door and shouting to catch me. I ran to the back and disappeared into the woods.

I underestimated the darkness of the night, especially in the wood. Nothing was visible. But I continued to run, flapping my hands around due to the big branches blocking my way.

The voices were not far from behind me. Then, I heard a gunshot. I started hyperventilating even more. This couldn't be how I die. No one was going to find my dead body. I'd be like that corpse I got acquainted with earlier!

My phone! I reached for my phone. It had the recording in it. I would not let that fall into their hands.

I halted for a second and patted the trees around.

I finally found a tree that was hollow inside.

Without thinking, I dropped it into the tree and continued to run. The men were behind me. I could see some torches. From my calculations, there were around four or five men. But thank God, I didn't hear another gunshot.

The path was going more downward as I went on. As I turned around to check who was following me again, I tripped on a tree root and spiraled down the path, hitting stones, pebbles, and trees everywhere.

At the last hitting point, I felt my head slammed hard against a rock, and there I went, falling into the water.

I don't even know where the water came from. I felt dizzy as I resurfaced from the water, seeing everything blurry. It must be the effect of spiraling down like this.

I looked around and noticed that it was a river. The water level reached my chest. It was quite deep. I spotted an old bridge some meters away and moved into the water, approaching it. Maybe I could get up, cross over it and continue running away.

My plan soon dissolved when I heard the men approaching. As quickly as I could in the water, I moved and positioned myself under the bridge, right in time as the men crossed over the bridge. The flowing water muffled the sound of my movements.

They paused for a moment over me, looking around.

"Damn it, where did that guy go?"

"Are you sure it was a guy?"

"It could have been that girl as well who tailed you earlier."

"Yeah, we only saw them from the back, and the hoodie hid them well."

"We should confirm it."

"Let's just continue searching for now. Boss won't be happy if he finds out."

I waited for them to be completely gone before I got out on the water. I was completely soaked and shivering. The night winds were very cold, especially as they hit against the very wet me.

No longer sure where I was or where to go, I followed the river's flow. I must have walked for fifteen minutes before finally seeing a small house. Maybe I was already near a town or something.

But other than the house, there was nothing in sight. I approached the house's yard. I should ask for help.

And yet again, my plan got interrupted as I saw a familiar black car approaching. Out in the open, I could be spotted easily. I looked around and saw a dog kennel. Why do I look so desperate? That's what I thought as I crawled into the dog kennel just in time as the car stopped on the narrow road in front of the house.

What is not gone unnoticed is my uninvited self in someone else's house, someone whose sleep was interrupted by the impolite me. Next to me was a very much awake dog, a Border Collie, who was looking at me with narrowed eyes and growling. Please, don't go woof!

I urgently searched in my pants' pockets for the occasional biscuits I stuffed inside. Finally, I successfully got a biscuit in my hand. I tried to silently tear the plastic and handed the biscuit to the dog. It looked at me with suspicion though he had already stopped growling at the sight of the snack.

I put the snack beside it and reached out to pat its head. It must have sensed no danger as it stuck out its tongue and gobbled the biscuit in one second.

My attention went back outside, where two men got out of the car. They were already at the door knocking, just a few steps away from me.

The door opened, and I heard them speaking to an older woman. They asked if anyone was there, and the old lady said no. They went away quickly, probably being pressured to find me. I wish I could laugh at their face, but here I am, praying for my safety as well.

As the car drove away, the dog barked happily at me. It approached me, sniffing around for another biscuit. I tried to silence it but couldn't. The door opened again.

"Millie?" the lady called out, approaching the kennel. She probably wasn't expecting my head to pop out with a 'hello' instead. She stepped backward with a shocked gasp.

"I'm sorry," I chuckled nervously, "I was just passing by."

After the old lady calmed down, I explained my situation about encountering some gang in the area. I made the poor, traumatized face to her, hoping she'd buy it. Upon noticing my shivering self, she invited me in, but I declined, saying I was a bit pressed to get away from the danger around here.

"Perhaps you know a small empty cabin around the woods? I left my bike there, but then I got lost."

"Oh yes. If you go down this road, there will be a narrow path to the left. It's along that path. And when you continue on that path, you'll reach the freeway back to Hertfordshire. But be careful not to encounter any more of these goons."

Thanking her, I ran along the road while being on the lookout for any other man running after me. Finally, I got a hold of my bike and wasted no time going away.

By the time I arrived at the front of my apartment, I was still shivering. The heavy weight of wet clothes on me didn't help the case. I was now very drowsy, and my eyesight was blurry. I felt like

I'd lose consciousness any second now. Damn, why would I be feeling sleepy right now at all times?

As I made my way up to my apartment on the third floor, I felt something sticky by the side of my face. My hand touched my face, and there was definitely some sticky liquid.

As I looked closely, it seemed red, almost like...blood!

My eyes widened at the sight of the blood plastered on my face until it almost reached my neck. When did that happen?

I needed to go up fast and get rid of the blood. I took a step forward, and I took a step back again. I hid behind a column in the parking lot.

Two men were passing by. I couldn't see them well because of the dark and the fact that they wore caps that hid half of their face. And their conversation seemed suspiciously about me.

I saw her car parked around there.

"We should still check her apartment to confirm for sure she isn't that person."

"You think she could be that person back there?"

"I wouldn't know since I had never met her before. The Doctor simply called me to check and confirm. But I don't think a girl would end up there, that too alone."

And their conversation became less clear as they went away. Or towards my apartment, that is. I couldn't go now. I needed to call Eli, so I searched for my phone but got nothing. Then I remembered. Ughh, what do I do now?

Oh, Brian! I was supposed to go there. I looked at the time. It was 8 pm. That was not too late. I could still go. I staggered to my bike. I would be able to reach there in ten minutes.

I slid into the elevator and sat down. I was so sleepy. I might just go right away to sleep when I reach there.

I was so unaware of my surroundings that I even missed the floor on which he lived.

When I finally reached his floor, I literally crawled toward his place. I wanted to cry. I looked so stupid.

I was about to knock but a pain shot up in my head as I clutched it tightly. My head felt heavy, and the sticky blood was everywhere on my palm as I held my head.

From the end of the hall, I saw someone approaching. But my vision was blurred.

"Help me," I said. But it came out as a croaked whisper only.

Too heavy. I felt too heavy as I plopped down on the floor. I needed to take a nap.

I closed my eyes and fell backward, right in time to watch the individual rush forward and hold me, calling my name.

I tried to continue sleeping, but the constant ringing sound in my head wouldn't let me. I tried to shake off the noise, but it only became more annoying. I opened my eyes reluctantly. All I saw was white, though a bit blurry. I blinked a few times. Where was I?

The last thing I remember is falling unconscious in front of Brian's apartment. Where did I end up? I shuffled a bit and sat up. Pain shot up in my head as I grabbed it hard to stop. But there was something around my head. I felt the soft thing with my hands and realized my head was bandaged.

At the same time, I heard footsteps and looked up to see someone approaching. I squinted my eyes to see better. It was someone tall, but my eyesight was still blurry. As the man approached me, the light in front of me was covered by his head, forming a halo around his head. I chuckled to myself. Is this an angel?

I kept staring at him until my sight became less blurry. When I could see clearly, I jumped back against the bed, clutching the bedsheet.

"Oh, devil!"

"Really now?" An amused voice shot back.

This tall guy with black hair and green eyes seemed awfully familiar, if I was not mistaken. A bit too familiar. Right, when I was about to speak, the door opened, and in came Eliyah with something in a paper bag. She threw it on my lap and sat on a chair beside the bed.

"You just woke up?" Eli asked with a blank face. Well, not a blank face; it seemed a kind of dark and threatening type of blank face.

"Yeah...the friend gathering went well, I assume?" I asked tentatively with an awkward smile, trying to ignore another stare next to her.

"We found you on the floor wet, shivering, with blood pouring down your head, unconscious. We dragged your stupid ass to the hospital. And we have been waiting for you to wake up for three hours. It is now midnight. That's all you can say?"

I pulled Eli by her sleeve to bring her closer to me and leaning on her shoulder, I whispered, "Yeah, but what is the devil doing here?"

She glanced to Castiel and then back to me. "You, my dear, owe your life to Castiel here. If he didn't arrive as late as you and didn't find you, I can't imagine how long you would have remained unconscious at Brian's door," she said smugly.

"Don't exaggerate," I murmured and scowled. Then I glanced at him and made sure to glare at him for him to receive the message clear: No, I don't owe you. Really though, we meet after all these years like this. Why like this?

Eliyah stood up and motioned Castiel to sit in her place. "You can sit down. I'll just call the doctor and come back." I tried to grab her hand but all I received in my hand was air. She practically flew out of the room. Well, her concern for me warms my heart.

Castiel slowly came over and sat down. I didn't look at him and nor did he look at me. He was just staring at his phone. There was an awkward silence. And I was getting thirsty. I coughed a bit. I coughed again. Then I coughed once more.

"Here," I heard and saw a glass of water placed in front of me. Without glancing sideways, I grabbed the glass of water. I gulped it all at once. I was so hungry as well. I reached for the paper bag and saw a burger in it. I've got such a good best friend.

As the burger was about to reach my mouth, I paused. I looked at Castiel. He was on his phone. I coughed to bring his attention right back to me. He glanced up, raising an eyebrow at me.

"Just for the record, I could have handled it alone. You didn't have to help me."

"Oh. I didn't intend to," he said like it was obvious.

"You didn't? Then why did you help me?" I asked surprised.

"Well, I was supposed to go to Brian's apartment. And you just happened to be blocking the way."

"Oh." Cue the embarrassment.

"Well, you could have just put me aside and entered," I said to myself under my breath.

"Anyway, I thought I was the one more likely to end up like this because of my job. Your job seems as much thrilling," he remarked dryly, looking me up and down. I looked down as well and noticed I got some cuts and scratches as well.

"Pfft, what would you know about my-"

His phone cut my sentence. He looked at his phone briefly and then looked at me. "Can I take this call?"

"Oh, you need my permission?"

"No, it was just a polite way of saying it," he said nonchalantly.

I took a deep breath and clenched my wrists. It had only been a few minutes and he was already driving me over the edge. Even my heartbeats became erratic, due to my suppressed anger for sure. This, in turn, was well reflected on the heart rate monitor beside my bed, which started beeping even faster. I blinked furiously at the monitor willing for it to disappear as my eyes went back to a very amused Castiel.

"What are you looking at? My heartbeats have always been a bit, uhm, energetic. Don't mind me and take your call," I snapped.

He shook his head, chuckling as he stood up. He took the call, walking to the window as he talked. I tuned out what he was talking about as I looked at him. It had been six years since I last saw him. He seemed more refined, no longer the boy I knew.

He must have let his hair grow more, I noticed, as his tousled black hair almost reached his neck. His face was stronger and more defined, giving him a serious manly look. I noticed that he was wearing a dress shirt which fitted him well and made his shoulders and muscles look more prominent. He was holding his suit jacket in one hand while his phone was in the other. Damn, he could make a girl blush if it was not for his attitude.

The entrance of the doctor brought me out of my thoughts. He was followed by Eliyah and Brian. "I see you've woken up. How are you feeling right now?"

"Oh, just a headache. And I'm feeling a bit dizzy. But I'm okay right?" "No, you're not. You've taken quite a blow on your head. You suffered a mild concussion."

"And I wonder how? Maybe while playing catch the criminal game?" Eliyah said as she crossed her arms, glaring at me.

"Oh, haha, yeah..." I trailed off ignoring her demonic expression.

"You need some rest, Miss Carter. At least a week. I've prescribed a few medicines for your headache and fatigue. For tonight, you should stay here," the doctor said and went out.

I sighed and looked at Brian who stood next to Eliyah. "Sorry. Not only was I late, I didn't even manage to get inside," I laughed to ease the tension.

"Yeah, funny right?" Eliyah asked chuckling. But it was the kind of chuckle that dared me to continue laughing and agreeing. Like one mom ain't enough...

"Handle your girlfriend, Brian. She's scary right now," I whispered to him. Sadly not low enough as Eliyah stomped towards me with death glares while Brian just grinned widely, grabbing Eliyah's hand holding her back.

"You! I just want to freaking knock your stupid head off!"

"No need. She did it to herself already," a snarky comment popped in. I rolled my eyes at Castiel who returned back to my side after his call.

Just then, Eliyah's phone started ringing. Damn, this made me remember my phone. It contained crucial evidence which I needed to fetch as soon as possible.

Eliyah took the call, spoke a few words and handed it to me. 'Attorney Kim', she mouthed to me. Oh, he must have been trying to call me.

"Hello, sir. I'm sorry, my phone is currently not with me." "I guessed so. I called to inform you that the case about Argan Gregore has been closed in case you were still working on it."

"What? How can the case be closed? Why so?" I asked as I straightened up in bed, while the others stood to attention, looking at me.

"That's because he has been found already. Dead by the road near some faraway village. He has been found two hours ago."

My heart started beating erratically. I'm sure this has something to do with me breaking into somewhere I shouldn't have been. Would I have ended up like this if those people managed to catch me?

I heard Attorney Kim speaking again. "No need to concern yourself with this case anymore. Anything with it now has been taken over by the IOF." "Wait, isn't it totally closed? Why is the IOF taking the case?" I asked glancing at Castiel whose attention perked up at the mention of the IOF.

"Your case was to do with Argan's disappearance but he has been found now."

"Yes, but I need to determine the reason-"

"That is not our concern. The case is supposedly linked to other recent cases that were being handled by the IOF. So it's no longer ours. You'll be assigned another one tomorrow at work. Good night."

"But-"

He ended the call. I let out a frustrated sigh. He never listened.

"Argan Gregore has been found dead," I informed Eliyah as I handed her back her phone.

I looked back at Castiel and snapped my fingers towards him. "Your organisation has taken my case from me," I said. I probably seemed childish but I felt offended that I'm being told not to meddle in it again. Like I even got a concussion and all these cuts for that case. If that ain't dedication, I don't know what is.

"Oh, that was your case?" he asked sounding surprised, "Well, it's better for the case to be handled by us since it's more important to us. This case is a clue to a larger case of ours." "Oh really. Elaborate please," I huffed and crossed my arms.

"No, that's confidential."

"You know I'm the one that possesses the most information on this current case, right?" I said. "What I went through a few hours ago says enough. I'd at least like to know how you'll continue on with this case."

He looked hesitant for a while, probably pondering on whether to tell me or not. "You'll know about it if you'll be contacted about the case."

I sighed and looked over at Eliyah. "Can you go to my apartment and fetch some clothes and toiletries?" I pleaded. "Please, please, my apartment is like only five minutes away by car from here. Go with Brian and then both of you can return home. I'm sure you all must be tired." I threw a convincing smile to Brian.

She threw an exasperated look at me. "You haven't even said how you ended up in this state, you know."

"I swear. I'll tell you in the morning. It's already late right now," I said, trying to look as firm as I could.

"But-" she started before Brian dragged her away and closed the door. And as they disappeared, an awkward silence crept into the room again. I kept playing with my fingers as a distraction, but after some long suffocating minutes, I couldn't restrain myself anymore. The awkwardness felt as if I was being strangled. I glanced at Castiel and found him staring back at me. I seized the chance to ask some questions brewing in my mind.

"So when will the autopsy be carried out? It needs to be done as soon as possible. That man may have been dead for several days."

"Oh really? How do you know that?" he asked suspiciously.

"I said 'may.' It is just a supposition. But is it really the case though?"

"Yes, it was a colleague who had called a while ago and told me about it," he looked at me as if trying to figure me out. I squirmed in my place and threw him an innocent smile.

Just then, his phone rang again. "Oh, it's Brian," he said, puzzled, and took the call.

He then put the phone on loudspeaker for me to hear as well.

"Lyn, you here?" I heard Eli's voice, which sounded a bit weird.

"Yes, what happened?"

"Did you, by any chance, forget to lock your apartment's door?" "No, not at all. I remember clearly that I locked it. Why?"

"I think...a burglar had come in your absence. Your living room is in disarray right now."

"Oh...well, okay. Just take my things and return back."

"Didn't you hear me? I said a burglar had broken into your apartment!" she exclaimed, waiting for me to react.

"Well, it's already done now. Just return quick."

I heard a confused okay, and they hung up.

"You seem to know what happened and who broke into your apartment," Castiel observed.

"Who said so?"

"Obviously, your reaction. This has to do with what happened to you, right? Just what mess did you end up in?"

I sighed inwardly. That guy was too smart for his own good. And he had the nerve to look so confident at me.

"Maybe, but that's none of your business."

Castiel smirked and looked away. Then he mumbled to himself. I was sure I heard something like still such a stuck-up girl.

"Conceited ass," I snidely commented while looking in the opposite direction and then looked back to see his reaction.

He was smirking at me. I looked at him weirdly.

"I've missed that," he said quietly.

"What? Those harsh facts that only I have the pleasure to remind you of? Any time, Castiel," I said, showing him my best fake smile.

Just then, Brian and Eliyah stormed in with my essentials. I took the bag and thanked them when Eliyah grabbed my shoulders and shook me. "A burglar, Haelyn, a burglar!"

"I doubt-"

"I wonder what they could have taken-"

"No, really though-"

"It could've been dangerous if you were"

"Don't worry."

"We need to report to the-"

"I know who it was."

Eliyah stopped mid-sentence and looked at me. "You know what?"

"It's all related. I'll tell you tomorrow. It's almost 1 a.m right now. You all need to go home."

"You put me through so much stress and suspense. How am I supposed to get any sleep now?" Eliyah complained.

"Just forget it for now. Time to say goodbye."

"Tomorrow, I'll squeeze every teeny-weeny detail out of you," she said and got out. "Good night, sweet dreams," I called after her as Brian followed after.

I looked up at Castiel. "No good night or sweet dreams for you. Only nightmares. Bye."

He chuckled. "No nightmares, thank you. I don't want to dream of you."

Before I could retort back, he was out of the room. Aghh, I'd get him back another time.

The next morning, I headed to my apartment for some minutes and changed into my working clothes. The state of my apartment left me speechless. Whoever did this was going to pay dearly.

I headed to the law firm shortly after. What was embarrassing was the large bandage wrapped around my head that caught pretty much everyone's attention. I brushed off their questions, saying that I simply fell down at home and hit my head.

For now, I had to go to Attorney Kim's office. As usual, I found his head buried under stacks of files on his table. I knocked and entered.

"Here you are-" he stopped midway in astonishment staring at me. "What did you get yourself into?"

I sat in front of him and waited for him to snap out of his daze. I was about to open my mouth when I heard a knock, and Eliyah entered the office. "I thought we were supposed to meet first thing in the morning."

"Well, you came at the right moment. I was just about to-"

Another knock interrupted us. It was another employee. "Haelyn, you're requested into the meeting room. Eliyah and Mr. Kim as well."

I stared at Attorney Kim questioningly. "What is this about?"

He pursed his lips and stood up. "Let's go. You'll find out soon."

We walked out of his office, Eliyah and I following behind him, wondering what was going on. We took the lift up to the seventh floor, where the meeting room and conference hall were situated.

Attorney Kim knocked on the door first and entered. We followed suit. There, in the meeting room, around the large circular table, sat ten men, all dressed head to toe in black. They could make people squirm with their looks. They were so unnerving. They all looked stoic, guarded, and serious.

Well, not all. One among them was sending me an annoying smirk as a greeting.

"Oh, hello, come in. You've arrived at the right time. Take a seat," I heard Mr. Lawson say as he stood at the table side, near the door.

Attorney Kim shook hands with him and sat down while Eliyah and I walked around awkwardly and took the seats farthest from the scary-looking men. From what I could see, Castiel seemed the youngest out of them all. I tried my best not to glance at any of the men around the table and instead focused on Mr. Lawson.

"Since the people you needed have arrived, I'll be going," Mr. Lawson said as he smiled at us and nodded at the other gentlemen. Why was he going already? Way to make it awkward.

As he closed the door, a silence filled the room. I shared subtle glances with Eliyah and looked down at my lap. Should we be saying hi or something?

One of the men coughed to gain everybody's attention and stood up. He seemed to be in his fifties, but he was still as built as the others. He carried himself with an air of prestige and power. He must be the one who held the highest post of authority among the men present here.

"Allow me to introduce myself. My name is Aaron Ford, the Deputy Director of the UK's International Operation Forces headquarters," he said with a serious face.

I leaned towards Eliyah. "Should we be standing up and introducing ourselves as well?" I whispered.

"No," I heard from my left side, where Attorney Kim was seated. I guess I need to improve my skills at whispering. He gave me the 'let-me-do-the-talk' look. "Nice to meet you, Mr. Ford. I heard that your team took over the recent case that was under my responsibility. I believe the police have already sent you the files concerning the case. Is there a reason why your team has come here?"

"Yes," Mr. Ford said and continued, "we need all information about the case, and the police files about Argan Gregore are not enough. Since it was a recent case of your firm, I believe your team may be the ones who hold the details. I need all interview and investigation reports. I need your cooperation. So can I meet with your team?"

"That's me," I raised my hand proudly.

Mr. Ford looked at me and nodded. "And who else?"

"Me," I raised my hand again.

"Yes, you just said so. But who else?"

"Me. Only me," I said like it was obvious.5 "Then, you must be good at your work, right?" someone else asked. Someone who I'd rather shut up.

"None of your concern," I grumbled and glared at Castiel.

"Actually, Miss, it is somewhat important to us since we have taken over the case, and we need all the information related to it, including previous interviews and investigations," someone else interjected while Castiel smirked smugly. I would have glared at the other man as well, but his face seemed to tell me to refrain from that.

"Too late," I said and crossed my arms.

"What do you mean, Miss?" Mr. Ford said darkly, raising an eyebrow at me.

"Carter. Haelyn Carter. And what I mean is that the files are no longer in my hands. I'll have to rewrite a report if you need information, which could take some time."

"What do you mean you don't have the files?" snapped Attorney Kim beside me.

"Not my fault it was stolen," I mumbled, scowling.

Everyone leaned forward, and ears perked up in attention. "Stolen, damn it! The files were stolen yesterday night while I was at the hospital. I searched for the files to bring to the office a while ago at my apartment, but there was no trace of any paper or file linked to Argan Gregore."

There was a chorus of sighs around the table.

"Now, what do we do?" I heard another man ask, tilting his head in annoyance.

"As I said, I will write another report. I'm taking full responsibility," I replied in a clipped tone. Though this wasn't my fault, well, partly, I felt like I added to their trouble.

Mr. Ford pressed both palms on the table and sat down. "It's okay. No need to waste your time over it. Just give us a recap of everything you can remember," he said and gestured to another man, who took a laptop out of I don't know where.

So I ran through all the interviews and places I went to, including all people I suspected. And then, I arrived at the part of yesterday's incident. Taking a great breath, I started narrating what happened yesterday, which got a bit more attention. And Eliyah continued describing my apartment's condition after the break-in of last night.

"Where was the place you went to specifically?"

"Well, I'm not sure. I had taken the road towards Hertfordshire. But I don't think I did enter Hertfordshire. It was probably somewhere like Weaton," I thought as I frowned in concentration, trying to remember.

"Interesting. Argan Gregore's body was found near Stradshill, which is just a few kilometers away from Weaton," mused one of the men.

"We need to go there first. I don't think there will be anything there, though. Since there was an intruder, they'll be sure to evacuate as soon as possible, which they may have already done," Mr. Ford inserted.1 "And, Miss Carter, you are currently a witness to our case. From what you said, I believe you may not be safe at your place. From chasing you, shooting at you, or entering your apartment, this all shows to what extent your life is in danger," Mr. Ford said sharply.

I gulped as I grasped the reality of my situation. They could come to my place again and finish me once and for all. But they did not even know for sure that it was me.

"God! What do I do?" I whispered to myself in a frantic tone and slammed my head on the table.

"Uhh," Castiel coughed and turned to Mr. Ford, "so should we be putting her under the Witness Protection Program?"

This caught my attention. I glanced up. "What is this about?"

"This program is to ensure the security of any threatened witnesses during any of our cases. This suits your situation right now. I suggest that you move out for a while."

"But where will I be living then?"

"You can stay with me," Eliyah inserted with a worried look.

"Oh, ye-" I started.

"No," Castiel interrupted.

"No? What do you mean 'no'?" I asked, perplexed. "Those people already know your identity. They'll search for you, and you could be putting others' lives in danger if they find you."

"So what are you hinting at? I go homeless?"

"Well, that wouldn't be a bad idea," he thought it over with a serious face, though I could see the amusement in his eyes.

Seeing my 'no-nonsense' face, Mr. Ford said, "The IOF owns many apartments around here where the employees stay. If you are under the Witness Protection Program, you can stay there or with the Special Agent that is appointed to protect you."

"Oh, interesting. So when do I move?"

"After signing this paper," said the man who was typing on the laptop as he took a paper out of a file and slid it over to me. "This paper is to be signed by the witness, acknowledging all the services we will be giving and agreeing to cooperate with us," he explained.

Well, there's nothing to lose, I thought as I grabbed a pen and signed it.

"Okay, you can go to your apartment and collect your necessities. We'll make sure someone accompanies you, just in case."

"Thank you, and concerning the case, I have some recordings on my phone, which could be very helpful. I recorded men's conversations at that warehouse," I said as I slid the paper back to the man.

"Oh, really?" Mr. Ford exclaimed, surprised. "You should have said so earlier. Where is it?"

"Uhm, well, that's the problem. I left it back there in the woods while running away. And it's a good thing I did because it would have been damaged if I had kept it with me when I fell in the water. I guess I have to go with you back there again," I proposed.

Mr. Ford thought it over for a while and then agreed. "Since you know the exact location, then maybe it's better for you to go."

"Okay, I guess that will be all for now. Let's go now, guys!" I said, standing up and getting ready to go. Everyone just stared at me. I regained my professional composure and offered, "With your permission, that is."

"I bet you will become a stone-like them in some years," I whispered to Castiel.

He gave me a blank stare in turn.

"Oh, good job! You're already halfway there!" I exclaimed.

I believe that sitting in a car with three Special Agents is no easy work. The two agents in front didn't even introduce themselves, so I named them Cooky and Shooky for no good reason whatsoever.

The air felt so stuffy with the silence, though. I tried making casual talks, but no one bothered to reply. Well, bummer. I didn't know I was such a nuisance.

Thankfully, the journey was not that long. Day and night were so different. I realized that when I tried to give the exact location. I made them stop at the end of the unpaved road and got out.

I glanced around to make sure we had arrived at the right place. That was it. The woods looked less scary during the day, but I could recognize them well.

My scary friends soon joined me by my side. Actually, they just passed by me and started walking right ahead.

I grunted and strutted behind. Watching the agents decked in classy suits and shoes walking along a muddy path in the middle of the woods was surely an unusual sight. But they just continued walking as if they could care less.

I ran beside Castiel. "Give me your phone," I demanded, stretching my hands forward. He raised an eyebrow at me as he continued walking.

"I don't remember where I hid my phone, so I'm gonna try calling from yours," I explained.

He sighed and took out his phone from his pocket. He unlocked it and handed it over to me. Then I remembered something and stopped.

"You guys continue along the path, and you'll find the old warehouse. The tree where I dropped my phone is somewhere along the river, so I'll continue to the woods until I see the river," I proposed.

The three stopped and looked at each other, thinking about what to do. In the end, Castiel nodded at Cooky and Shooky, who continued walking while Castiel turned back and walked towards me. I looked at him questioningly.

"Someone needs to keep you safe," he said in an unconcerned manner and started walking ahead of me toward the woods.

I walked behind him. "Aww, thanks. What a gentleman!" I cooed and was going to pat his head, but he slapped my hand away, scowling. "I had no choice," he mumbled.

I followed Castiel as he took the lead. He seemed to know where he was going, professionally dodging all branches and roots in his way. And I was behind, all branches kissing my face and the roots violently greeting my feet.

We finally reached the riverside, and I told him to continue walking until we reached the bridge. When we approached the bridge, I dialed my number and called. I could hear my ringtone blasting somewhere among the peaceful, silent trees.

"It's somewhere in the northwest direction. It's a big tree with a hollow trunk," I informed Castiel. He nodded and walked in that direction. It was easy to spot the tree. I ran there and stuck my head inside. I grabbed my phone and stood up. I checked carefully to make sure it was not broken or something.

I put it in my jacket pocket. I was going to hand Castiel his phone when I looked at it again.

"Oh wait, I'll delete my-"

"No time. We need to hurry," he said as I felt the phone disappear from my hand.

We hurried over to the abandoned building and reached there in only a minute. The warehouse looked more repulsing during the day than at night. I could now comfortably walk around without worrying about the noise I was making.

Shooky was holding a camera and taking pictures around. There was no sign of Cooky. He was probably inside. I went in from the front door, which made a screeching sound as I pushed it open. Hmm, well, there wasn't really anything to see here.

I passed by the room into which I had entered from the window. I put my head in and immediately retracted. The awful smell still lingered. I almost jumped when I felt someone tapping my shoulder.

"Move," I heard as Cooky entered, almost pushing me aside.

"This is the room in which Argan Gregore's body was kept," I commented, trying to sound smart, as Cooky took photos while looking around.

"No, it wasn't," I heard from behind me.

"What do you mean? I was here yesterday and saw the body," I scoffed at Castiel, who almost passed by and entered the room.

"Did you see his face?"

"Well, no, but-"

"Then, don't be so certain about it."

Cooky nodded in agreement at Castiel and left the room. "Time to go," Castiel said as he went out, with me following, mouth agape at their blatant rudeness.

Throughout the ride back to the new apartment where I'd be living temporarily, I kept glaring at Castiel. I really hoped I was bothering him.

Finally, after great efforts, he looked at me. "What?" he asked.

"It's rude to disregard someone's words like that."

"No, I'm just disregarding a wrong opinion."

"How so?" I argued, crossing my arms and turning to him.

"The autopsy results state otherwise, that's how."

"It's already out?" I asked, surprised.

"No, only some basic information was given. The time of death was said to have been around two days ago. He was assumed to have died from excess bleeding from a knife wound."

I remained silent as I contemplated the idea. "What about that other corpse, then?"

"From the stench, it seems obvious that he has been dead for more than a week and was there for a while."

"But when I was spying on them, one of the men entered with a corpse. Does that mean-"

"Yes. There was more than one body. It could be only two or more. The warehouse, despite its appearance, was being used for a while now."

We arrived at the apartment after a long hour ride. I got out of the car pulling a small suitcase along with me. I took a small breath and glanced up at the tall building. Around it was a cluster of similar buildings that probably belonged to the organization.

The exterior look was like that of a hotel, light cream colored while evoking a classy modern image. The building had at least twenty floors, all with sliding glass doors leading to a small, nice-looking balcony. Hmm, it would have been cool if I could get an apartment for myself here.

By the time I finished analyzing where I'll temporarily be staying, the other three agents were already going inside. They either forgot that they had to show me where I'd be staying or did not care.

I dragged my suitcase and rushed to their side as we took the elevator. Cooky got off on the second floor, while Shooky got out on the fifth one. Should

I follow Castiel when he also gets off the elevator? He didn't tell me anything yet.

The elevator's door opened on the seventh floor, and Castiel got out. I was going to open my mouth when I saw him taking my suitcase with him. I followed behind silently.

We reached an apartment with the number 66 on the door. He put my suitcase down beside the door. "Judy Winter. That's the name of the agent assigned to protect you and with whom you'll be staying. Mr. Ford thought you may be more comfortable with a girl to stay by your side."

With that said, he walked to the end of the hall and went into the last apartment to the left. I made a grimace as I stared at the door. Did I have to do this alone? That was so awkward, I thought as I knocked on the door. I reassured myself that since it was a girl, maybe she would be more friendly compared to the other scary-looking men.

The door opened. I was going to say hello, but I didn't get a chance as the girl left the door open for me to enter and walked away.

I walked in hesitatingly with a stunning face as my eyes followed the girl who went to the kitchen. She seemed quite tall, around 5'9 ft, with a black bob hairstyle. She seemed so intimidating, definitely older than me. Perhaps I had thought wrong; she had no friendly vibe.

I approached her and cleared my throat a bit. "Hi, I'm Haelyn Carter," I introduced myself while giving a tentative smile and offering my hand.

She was mixing something in a blender and glanced up at me for the first time. No smile on her face. She looked at me up and down in a seemingly judging way, and her eyes returned to my face again. "I know. Your room is to the left," she said, and her eyes went back to the blender.

Okay, no handshake. My hand returned to my side awkwardly. I turned around, grabbed my suitcase, and headed to my room.

I opened the door and entered. I put my suitcase near the bed and glanced around. The room was plain white and seemed bare, with only a bed, a wardrobe, and a small table beside the bed. Anyway, it didn't matter since I'd stay here for only a short time, I hoped.

I opened my suitcase and took out the files I had dumped in it in a rush. I needed to get back to work now. I walked out of the room, closed the door, and passed by the kitchen when I heard Judy speaking on the phone.

"-but I really wanted to go with the team back to Canada. Instead, I'm stuck babysitting someone who can't protect herself."

Oh...

Okay, don't be judgemental.

Don't be judgemental.

Don't be a judge- Wow, what a bitch.

With a sigh, I quickly passed by without her noticing. I got out of the apartment and headed to the elevator. I pitied her, really. She did not know the honor she got for being the one chosen to protect me.

I planned to go to work, but I ended up going to a burial instead, that of Argan Gregore.

After the autopsy was done, the body of Argan Gregore was handed over to a funeral home which took the responsibility of burying him.

Except for the funeral home workers and me, no one else was present. It was a bit surprising that no people came. I mean, I thought there would at least be some family members or past friends that would come.

The only reason I was present at the burial was to meet Argus. I heard that he was informed of the death of his brother, so I thought that maybe I should talk to him about what happened to him.

So after the burial was finished, which included no funeral ceremonies at all, I stayed behind waiting for Argus. He was probably somewhere far since he seemed to be late. But then, Argan's death was informed to him yesterday itself.

I stood under a tree near the grave of Argan. I stared at his gravestone. It had only his name. His grave was bare, with not even a flower. Well, what a lonely death.

I was unaware of how long I stood there until I heard my phone ringing. It was Eliyah.

"Are you still at the graveyard?"

"Yeah. I don't know why but Argus has not come yet. I called his phone but didn't get him." "I was just informed that yesterday when they called him, they found out that he was using his friend's number here. His friend said that he was no longer in England but had returned to Italy. So come back. You went there in vain."

"Why would he return after filing a case for his brother? A case that is still ongoing?" I asked, confused. This did not make sense.

"I thought so as well. Maybe there was an emergency. Anyways, return soon. And Attorney Kim told me to pass his message to you: Stop wasting your time with useless things. It is still work hours," Eli said, laughing.

I chuckled as well. "Tell him to get my new case ready then."

"Actually, from what I can see, a pile of files is on your table right now."

He's too fast. I thought as I sighed.

"Here, I bought coffee for you as well," I said as I handed it over to Eliyah and sat down.

"I can only see the tip of your head from that pile of files," Eliyah said and laughed after I sat down. "Sharing is caring. Want some?" I said, popping my head out of the pile with a fake smile.

Nah, I'm good.

Paperwork; the nightmare of all employees. I clapped my hands and took a deep breath.

"So, where do I start?" I mused as I stared so lovingly at the files.

"Maybe with the drafting of the meeting procedures. Some are needed for tomorrow. They are all for this week's meetings. Then you can continue with the depositions and finish the report preparations," Eliyah advised.

"Thank you! What would I be able to do without you, my savior?" I exclaimed, my hands reaching out to her dramatically for effect.

I grabbed my laptop and the first file while discarding the rest aside. "I can't handle the sight of all these files. Half of them are not even for Attorney Kim. Am I being paid for these additional works?" I thought aloud.

"Actually, Eric has quit. So his workload has been distributed to some of us. You'll be paid for the additional work," Eliyah confirmed.

"You mean that's only a part of it? He has obviously been neglecting his work, and now I have to bear his burden."

"Didn't you know? He actually was in love with Diana, you know, the assistant from the other department? She's his ex, and he came here to try to convince her to be back with him. Then, he found out that she had left him because she had found another boyfriend. He quit with a broken heart," Eliyah explained as she shook her head in sympathy. "Oh, poor him...," I started, but then my eyes fell on the files, "but still, work is work. Work neglect is unacceptable and unprofessional."

I started working on the files right away. It seems like I will be stuck till late in the office itself today.

"I need the medical report of a past patient admitted at the Wellsworth Hospital. It concerns the drug case about which we'll have a meeting tomorrow," informed Attorney Kim while flipping through the papers I had prepared.

It was already evening. After hours of typing, I finally finished my work for the day. Or maybe not, from what I just heard.

"So, I need to go to the hospital? Because from what I saw, there was no official medical report in the file," I said.

"Yes. And keep it with you and bring it tomorrow when you come to work." Phew, at least!

I got in my car and threw my bag on the seat beside me. I hoped I won't have to wait for hours like in my past experiences.

I started the car and drove at a leisurely pace. I was in no hurry to go to my new place. It didn't have a friendly vibe. I wished I could have stayed with Eliyah, though it would be awkward sometimes since Brian often came over to her apartment.

I parked my car and got out after searching for the file I needed inside my bag, or the black hole, to be more specific.

I entered the hospital and went directly to the administrative office.

"Good evening. I need the medical record of a past patient called Samuel Johns," I said, showing the employee the necessary papers.

He nodded and went to his computer while asking another employee to fetch a file.

"It will take a few minutes. You can wait outside," he informed me. I thanked him and went out.

I saw a nurse passing by and smiling at me as I waited outside. It was the nurse whom I talked to the last time I came here. I returned her smile.

"We meet again. Are you here for the case you asked me about the other day?" She asked as she approached me.

"No, actually, it's no longer my case. It has been transferred to another team. I'm here for some papers I needed for another case," I replied.

"Oh. I wanted to say something about the previous case, but it may not matter now. Anyway, good luck with your job," she said as she turned to walk away. But, of course, I could not let her walk away.

"No, wait! Tell me what you want to say. Maybe it could be useful information. I'll relay it to the people that are responsible for the case now."

"Actually, it's no big thing. I just wanted to say that last time, you asked me to identify a man from that photo, right? But after that day, I saw him only once at the hospital."

Oh...interesting...

"But you said he works at the hospital, right?"

"That's what I concluded since I had seen him in male nurse clothes a few times. I thought maybe he was a new one here. I saw him for the first time only a few weeks ago. So I could have been wrong as well. I'm not sure."

"Thank you for the information. It'll be very helpful.

I'll inform those responsible for the case."

She nodded and walked away. As for me, I was drowning in my imagination and theories. More investigation should be done on that guy. After all, wasn't he the one whose car I chased till we reached an abandoned building with dead bodies? Or was it the other one? There were initially two men involved on the day that Argan disappeared.

Just then, I saw Dr. Martinez passing by and entering the administrative office. Oh, my luck!

I heard him asking one of the employees to get some papers ready. I stood by the door, waiting for him. As he stepped outside, he took a step back, surprised when he saw me.

"Hello again, Doctor," I said, grinning as I casually leaned against the wall.

"I thought we were not to cross paths again. Really, I don't have any time for you," he said grimly.

"Oh, no need to fret. I'm not here for you. But anyway, how have you been, Doctor?" I said with a seemingly polite smile. On the inside, I was cackling. I don't know why but I liked getting on the nerve of some people. People that tried to shove their attitude in my face.

He didn't answer and just stared at me.

"Oh, you won't talk? It's okay. I talk enough for two," I said and shrugged.

"You heard about the case, right? If you keep updated with the news, you must have seen or heard it. Argan Gregore was found dead," I said and waited for him to react.

He merely shrugged and said, "Well, that's unfortunate. I wonder what kind of gang-related activities he fell into to have died like this."

"What do you mean?" I asked as I straightened up my posture.

"He had stimulant drugs trafficked inside the prison, which he used to take. These were the cause of his heart attack. So if he ran away back to the gang that supplied him with the drugs or ended up in some bad situations, he had only himself to blame."

"And how did you come up with these assumptions? Are you sure you don't know anything?"

"It seems like you doubt me, Miss Carter. But your doubts are groundless, while my assumptions are solely based on what I know. He was a prisoner and drug addict whose case almost harmed this hospital's image. And he died outside of the hospital in God knows what situation. He's of no concern to me now."

"We'll see about that, Dr. Martinez, because it seems to me that there may be something fishy here. For now, I can only doubt it. However, try to hold onto your dear hospital's image while I gather the necessary evidence," I said. What was I rambling about? That case ain't even mine.

He rolled his eyes and was about to retort back when he was interrupted.

"Dr. Martinez, aren't you supposed to be going for the scheduled surgery right now? Your team is waiting for you," I heard from behind Dr. Martinez.

I glanced behind him. It was another doctor. He must be in his mid-thirties. He was wearing a white coat over his doctor scrubs and had blond hair slicked back.

"Yes. Someone insignificant held me back. I'll be going. Take the papers that we need from here later," he said and quickly walked away towards the operation unit.

I rolled my eyes and looked away as I continued waiting. But the doctor in front of me didn't walk away. I looked at him with a questioning face.

"You're Haelyn Carter, the one who was investigating a case here? Martinez mentioned it," he said with a smiling face.

"Yes...and who are you?"

"I'm Dr. Alex Sullivan, as you can see," the man said, gesturing to his name on his white coat.

"Oh, okay. Nice to meet you."

"I apologize for Dr. Martinez's words. I've been here for only a few months, but I am already used to Dr. Martinez's uhh, how should I put it?"

"Barbaric manners? Rudeness? Arrogance?" I offered.

"Yeah, that," Dr. Sullivan said, chuckling. "He's mostly like these concerning things he doesn't care about. Meaning everything besides his job." "You could maybe advise him on changing his attitude. It's not professionalism if that's what he calls it."

"Oh, I don't think a newbie can advise a senior about this, and he is a bit intimidating." He let out an awkward laugh, scratching the back of his neck.

"I'd volunteer to do it nicely. Though he does seem cold and mysterious, don't you think so?"

"Well yeah, he likes to be lonely and doesn't speak that much to anyone. He does have the mysterious, dark vibe," Dr. Sullivan said.

"Like how dark? So dark that he could do something bad or illegal?" I asked, probing deeper.

"Yes, he could," he said seriously and then laughed at my facial expression, "I'm joking. He cares too much about his job to do anything that will make him lose his job."

"Okay, if that's what you say," I nodded slowly.

"You must have had to put up with him during your case investigation? Has it gone well, though?" he inquired.

"Unfortunately, the case is no longer mine. I don't know how it's going," I sighed. Though I will likely be sticking my nose in that business again soon.

"Oh really? Who has it been transferred to?" he asked, surprised.

"Uhm, well, to another organization, I believe," I said, trying not to reveal anything. I hesitated since the IOF usually does not reveal much to the public, so they may not like me doing so.

"Oh, I hope they resolve the case soon, then. It could damage Wellsworth's reputation if it goes on longer," he said, and I nodded in agreement.

"By the way, is your head okay?"

I looked at him, puzzled. Then he pointed to the medical gauze still wrapped around my head. "That? It's okay now, just some slight headaches surfacing now and then," I replied, touching the bandage over the gauze. I'm used to it now, so I sometimes forget it is in my head.

"If I may ask, how did it happen?"

"I slipped in the forest. I am quite clumsy," I answered.

"Oh, you shouldn't be going into forests first. Such walks or runs do not always end nicely for some people," he advised seriously.

"Agreed. It won't happen again."

Just then, the phone that was in Dr. Sullivan's hand started ringing. Both of us glanced down.

"I need to take this call. It was nice talking to you. Maybe we'll meet another day again and have a chat again," he said apologetically and walked away, taking the call.

I shrugged to myself. Well, he was nice. We could talk some other time again. It was good to create contacts in other fields as well. They could always come into use.

"Is it not finished yet?" I asked as I walked into the administrative office. I was sure a lot of time had passed by.

"Almost done. I just finished printing the papers, along with a few others. So it took some time to gather and separate each. There you go," the man said, handing me the papers and the file I gave him. Thanking him, I walked back to the parking lot.

I got into my car and kept the file in my bag to avoid mixing it with my other files. I was about to go out when I saw a car approaching. I waited for it to pass by.

As the car passed, I felt like I saw a familiar face. Brown curly hair, angular face with green eyes. If it weren't for Argus being in Italy now, I would have thought this was him. Anyway, I have seen him only once, so it was easy to be mistaken as it did.

I started my car and headed to the apartment. Why couldn't they give me an apartment to myself? Either way, I'll be paying, I thought as I sighed.

But I was good, as long as I did not see my 'babysitter's face.

As I entered slowly, not to make any sound, I got welcomed by the sight of three people in the living room: Judy, Castiel, and a stranger. They didn't seem to have a good expression on their faces. I should perhaps avoid them.

I got on my knees and crawled behind one of the sofas with one hand around my bag. When I arrived at the end of the sofa, I considered the strategies and ways to slip into my room without them noticing.

"Are you quite finished with whatever you're trying to do?" I heard from above, or more like from the sofa. Wait, the sofa can speak?

But it sounded more like Castiel's voice. Was he speaking to the others? Because I was sure they didn't notice me coming in. Well, I should confirm, at least.

I popped up my head in between Castiel and the stranger.

"Are you talking to me?" I asked in a whispering voice. I didn't know if I should be flattered, but my face scared the crap out of the stranger, who almost cracked his neck from turning around and moving away so fast.

"Can you please act like a civilized human for once?"

I stood up and scowled. I was going to continue towards my room when I heard Judy's voice.

"Sit down. We need to talk."

I took a step back and plopped on the sofa.

"You mean you need to talk. Okay, start. I'm listening," I said, crossing my arms.

Don't give me attitude seemed to be what Judy wanted to say from her facial expression.

"You know I've been assigned to protect you, right? This means I have to be by your side or know your whereabouts at all times. You just disappearing out of here is not the right way to act," she said in a patronizing manner.

I scoffed at her. She made me look like a teen who fled from home.

"Oh, so now you're concerned? It didn't seem like it when you were whining about getting a babysitting job," I said sarcastically.

Her eyes turned an ice-cold blue color as she glared at me. "Don't use that tone on me," she warned.

"Oh, I'd never!" I said with my mouth agape and hand over my chest. "My dad has taught me always to respect my elders."

I heard a muffled laugh from beside me. I glanced at the nice stranger and smiled.

"You're testing my patience," Judy said as she clenched her teeth. Well, she was one fiery person. Who would dare to mess with her? Oh, nope, definitely not me.

"Okay, don't start an argument now," Castiel intervened and turned to me, "you didn't inform her where you were going. You're in the wrong here."

"Excuse-"

"It is your security that matters right now, Haelyn, not who is responsible for it," he said coldly.

"Well, if you were so worried, you could have done it yourself," I mumbled silently to myself.

Castiel thankfully didn't hear and continued talking. "And protecting a witness is as important and dangerous as any other task handed over to us. The perpetrators may be keeping tabs on her right now.

I'm sure Mr. Ford would not want to know we are performing our tasks so half-heartedly," he said, indirectly firing nice remarks at Judy, who continued glaring at me like it was my fault.

Then he stood up, with the stranger standing up as well. "I hope you can sort it out between yourselves. Don't worry. I mean, don't bother me about it again. Raphael and I need to go now." "Yeah. Maybe we should meet up another time. And nice to meet you, Haelyn, I am Raphael. I live in the apartment right in front of you," he said and grinned as we shook hands.

"Can't you spare me a room at your apartment instead?" I whispered jokingly to him.

"Stop talking nonsense," Castiel said, pushing his way between us and dragging my newfound friend out.

I turned around and faced my roommate. "I kind of regret signing that paper now. Just give me your number. I'll give you updates on where I go. You coming along and protecting me is up to you."

And with that said, I headed to my room. I took out my phone. Time to call for pizza delivery. I don't think she'd feed me unless it were poison.

"A new case has been transferred to us. The file about the case is at the Eastern Police Station. You need to go fetch it," Attorney Kim said. "And this is the letter of transfer. Show it to them there," he added, handing me a paper.

"Right on it, Boss," I said and got out of his office. I texted Judy about where I was going to. I hated continuously sending her texts, so I just sent my weekly schedule at once. But then, I kept getting things to do and places to go that weren't on the schedule. So I had to bother her every time. Not that I hated bothering her, but I had to keep in mind that I had to text her.

It had been five days already. Five days full with only paperwork and no case investigation or interview at all. That was what a real paralegal job is. So boring. Why was I still waiting? I had to quit!

As I headed outside, I saw my car right in front of the firm instead of being in the parking lot. I grinned.

One advantage of getting a protector was getting a driver along with it. I got in the passenger seat and grinned at a grumpy Judy.

Ever since my apartment had been broken into by some 'mysterious' people four days ago for the second time, I had acquired a 24 hours protection service. So Judy has been dragged along with me to work. Not that she complained. I could not even get a word out of her. So as not to bother her so much, I usually returned to her apartment earlier and continued my work there itself.

On a side note, I became friends with Raphael, who I saw daily. I found out that he was also 24 years old, like me. That may be the only reason he became close friends with Castiel. Because how else can such a talkative and bright person befriend a stone?

While we talked daily, Castiel always managed to hinder the flow of conversation with remarks, all toward me. I didn't know why he always tagged along in the first place. He was probably jealous that I was stealing his best friend.

While I was in my thoughts, we arrived at the Police Station in no time. Judy got out with me. I muffled a smile. It felt like I had an assistant. The job she got probably had to be the most boring one she was ever given. Being at the law firm the whole day and just going to a few other places, there were few chances of anything happening to me in the middle of London.

So all she had to do was wander about with nothing to do. I tried sharing a few pieces of paperwork with her before, but her cold stare was most probably a negative response to my generosity. She was so cold. Maybe she took after her surname, Winter.

She followed me into the police station. We went into the main office, and I handed the paper to the Chief Officer. He asked for one of the constables to fetch the file as we waited.

Another officer came into the office and began talking to the Chief Officer.

My ears pricked up in attention as I heard the conversation sounding very interesting.

"Remember the prisoner who escaped with the help of some gang members from the prison a few weeks ago?" asked the officer while the Chief Officer nodded.

"Well, he has just been found dead," the police officer whispered.

"How so?" asked the Chief Officer, astonished.

The police officer started explaining. But because some other people were in the room, he spoke a bit more quietly.

I leaned forward and pressed my palms on the table. "I'm sorry, but can you please speak a bit louder? I can't hear," I whispered, breaking their conversation.

"Exactly why we are speaking quietly, Carter," the officer said, rolling his eyes. Since the beginning of my job, I have always been making trips between offices and police stations, so most of the officers knew me. And it was no surprise, but some of them did not like me. This officer seemed to be one of them.

"Well, I was just interested because it seemed similar to a case I had recently," I said and shrugged.

I guessed this grabbed the Chief Officer's attention.

He leaned forward. "What was the case about?"

"You must have heard of it. There was news on the prisoner Argan Gregore who supposedly escaped and had been found dead."

"Oh yeah, I read about it. What was the conclusion of the case?"

"Well, uhm...," I hesitated. I didn't know what was happening with the case, truthfully, "some more investigations have been carried out, and the rest of the information will be released soon, I believe. Right now, it's all confidential," I said, nodding strongly while Judy raised an eyebrow.

"Oh, you are still on the case, then?"

"No, she is," I said, gesturing to Judy beside me. Judy did not even refute my false claim. Both officers glanced at her. But the cold look that she was giving them made them refrain from asking further questions.

"So, what is the case about? Who is the prisoner? Who helped him escape? Was there a search team for him? When and where has he been found dead? Has the autopsy already begun?" I asked eagerly.

An officer approached me, "Your file, Miss," he said, handing it over. I grabbed it and put it on my lap. I looked back at the officers. "So?"

The officers looked at each other and glanced at Judy. She had a great presence with an intimidating vibe.

At least, she served a good purpose now.

"His name is Rick Walds. He was found exactly 30 minutes ago in some suburbs in East London. He escaped from prison three weeks ago. The investigation of his death has not started yet," said the officer.

"Ok, good then," I said, clapping my hands. The officers looked at me questioningly.

"Have a nice day," I said and stood up, ready to go.

As I walked outside, I took out my phone. I should call Raphael and inform him about this. It may be possible for the IOF to get the case responsibility before the police.

"Hello, Mr. Ford? There is some information that may be of interest to..." I heard from behind me. I looked behind and saw Judy passing by on her phone.

I just stood for a while, frowning and my mouth open. I sighed after a while and followed behind to my car.

Ugh, you rotten repugnant broccoli! Choco mint-flavored ice cream! Clout chasing lewdster!

I swear I'll get you back.

"So...that's the guy?" I asked, cocking my head, analyzing him. The man was sitting in the interrogation room while I was standing outside beside Castiel. In the IOF headquarters.

I was so happy that I got the incredible honor of seeing the inside of the IOF's UK headquarters. The exaggeration of me being very happy was solely because I got to be here; without Judy. She behaved like her normal self these past three days, acting as if she had done nothing wrong. Meanwhile, I was fuming each time I saw her face.

I even tried annoying her sometimes. Like yesterday, I added another 6 to her apartment's door. 666. Anyone passing by could tell who resided in it.

But what satisfied me at that time in the car was Mr. Ford's reply. "Okay, I'll get on it." That was it. Judy looked like she wanted to hear more, but poor her, she got only five words out of Mr. Ford, and that didn't even include a thank you or good job. I bit my cheeks at that time so as not to laugh.

But I refrained from letting her accompany me anywhere else. And even when I came here, I told her not to bother because I would already have Castiel by my side. Surprisingly, Castiel simply nodded and didn't give Judy any time to object. I simply hated him less sometimes.

Back to the subject, I continued analyzing the suspect. I was trying to see if he had the murderer's look. He was sitting alone in the interrogation room, with his handcuffs in one hand and the other clasped with the chair.

He was brought here yesterday, according to what Raphael told me. He was the suspect they got after taking the case in their hands. Meanwhile, Argan's supposed murderer was still unfound. Or the full team, that is.

"He was caught fleeing the prison a few hours after the escape of Rick Walds. But the interesting fact is that he was not a prisoner there. The officers there do not recognize him or know how he got in. That's why it was a bit difficult trying to track him. We assumed he helped Rick Wald escape, then fled right after." "Okay, but what are you waiting for? Interrogate him," I said.

"You think we didn't do it already?"

"Oh, you should have told me before, idiot. So what's the verdict?" I asked, turning towards him, meeting his glaring eyes. He didn't take casual insults lightly, but well, none of my concern.

He rolled his eyes and replied, "He refuses to speak English. He's Italian. We are waiting for another interrogator who's Italian. He'll be here in a few minutes."

"Pshh, you could have just told me to do it. Why wait?" I said, scoffing.

"I remember you having taken Italian classes in the first year of high school, Haelyn. A reminder; you failed."

"I know," I said, glaring at Castiel. "I just didn't pay attention. But this time, I'm better. I have google translate," I nodded smugly.[1] "I think a person itself may be more reliable than that," I heard from beside me as a man entered. Oh, it was Shooky. Damn, it's been a while since I saw him.

"Oh, you got the file on that guy? I thought you'd take more time," Castiel commented.

"Yup, there it is," Shooky said, approaching us with a file in his hands, "It was easy. I just ran his description in all police stations and got his information. I'll go in first and tell you later."

"Shooky, you're Italian?" I asked, surprised. He did not seem like one, and his accent was kinda normal. That is British normal.

Both men looked at me weirdly. Then I realized.

"Well, you didn't tell me your name...so I gave you one," I mumbled and shrugged.

"My name is Lucio," Shooky said in a hard tone. He didn't seem to appreciate nicknames.

"A bit too late now, don't you think, Shooky?" I grinned.

He opened his mouth and then shut it again. He turned around and got into the interrogation room.

He sat across from the suspect and put the file on the table. The suspect eyed the file, looked at Shooky, and slumped back in his chair in a laid-back manner. He looked a bit too at ease for me. How could anyone be like this in front of Shooky?

The interrogation started, but I couldn't understand anything. So I sat down and waited for it to finish. Finally, after fifteen minutes, the interrogation finished. Shooky came out and looked at Castiel. "We should discuss with the team a bit. Let him stay here for a bit till then."

"Okay, let's go," Castiel said, following Shooky. I started to move, but Castiel turned back, making my head collide with his chest. Damn, stone wall!

"You stay here. It's a confidential discussion," he said and got out, shutting the door.

I sat down with a frowning face. I felt like an outsider. Oh, wait...I was.

I looked around. There was nothing to do here. They may take a while with their discussion.

Then I noticed the file that Shooky left behind. A big smile erupted as I took the file in my hands. I was going to open it, but then I refrained and put it back on the table. They probably forgot it and will come to take it back.

I waited for ten minutes. No one came. I took the file again. This time, I opened it. The file had a lot of police reports and information about the suspect. Giuseppe Boccaccio. He's thirty years old. Oh! Is he an undocumented migrant? Interesting.

I flipped through the reports. He had gone in and out of police stations a few times before. I looked at him again. He was staring at the glass barrier. Perhaps he was wondering if there was someone here. Though he couldn't see me from inside, his stare made me uncomfortable.

I looked back at the file. He has been living in London for two years. Why would he refuse to speak in English? I narrowed my eyes at him again. He was definitely pretending. Should I tickle the answer out of him?

My hands were itching to do something stupid. I looked at the suspect then. He was still looking around, probably bored out of his mind. Maybe he needed a little chat.

I cracked my knuckles and grabbed the door handle. I opened the door to the investigation room. The suspect's head shot up, looking at me.

Trying to look as serious as I could, I took a seat. "Don't mind me. I'm only waiting for the rest to come. Why am I even explaining? You don't seem to speak English," I said and looked at him, waiting for his reaction. He just gave me a blank look. Oh, I see. Very well...

I leaned forward and slammed my hands on the table. "Stop pretending. I know who you are. You killed that man, right?" The suspect cocked his head at me as if confused. But I could see the amused look in his eyes.

"You helped that prisoner escape. But you also helped in his capture again, right? And let me guess. You and some other men took him to an abandoned building," I paused and looked at him. He straightened his posture with narrowed eyes at me. Good, I was on the right track.

"And you-"

Just then, the door slammed open. I jumped in my seat, thinking it was Castiel. I looked around just in time to see Raphael in front of me. He dragged me by the arm outside and shut the interrogation room's door.

"Are you crazy? You are not supposed to go inside! What if someone else caught you there? And that man is a suspect in a murder case. You realize that he is dangerous, right? Thank God I arrived first, or else you would have been kicked out of here by now," Raphael breathed out. A silence followed.

"Umm...I'm sorry?" I tried.

"What are you sorry for?" I heard Castiel's voice as he entered. Damn, the door was open! He looked like he didn't hear anything, though.

"I looked into the file, that's why," I said. I didn't lie. I only told half of the truth. I glanced at Raphael, silently asking for his cooperation. He scoffed at me but didn't say anything more.

Shooky followed inside with two other agents. They went inside. They were talking about something with the suspect. Then the two agents made him stand up, putting the handcuffs on both wrists, and took him out.

"Did you find him guilty? Where are they taking him?" I asked Castiel.

"He's an undocumented migrant. So, we are deporting him back to Italy."

"Bu-but isn't he a suspect in a murder case? You can't let him go free like that!" I exclaimed. They were not in their right mind.

Castiel and Raphael exchanged a look. They were hiding something from me.

Raphael shrugged. "Hmm, the IOF employees there will handle him. Let's go home now."

I was sitting at the back of the car, chatting with Raphael, who sat beside me. Castiel was driving in front with a scowling face. Poor boy, he got left alone in front.

Raphael told me about his training and work period in Turkey along with Castiel. At least he can speak a lot, compared to Castiel. I wouldn't be able to know all of this if I had asked Castiel instead.

"Oh, and I should totally show you some of the photos I took. I'm quite skilled in photography. I left my phone at home, so when we arrive, I'll show you," Raphael said, grinning. I nodded and smiled back.

"And while you're at it, you should also move back to your apartment. The A/C is working again now," Castiel inserted out of nowhere.

Raphael groaned. "Can't I just stay in yours from now on?" he asked.

"What do you mean?" I asked, confused, looking between them.

"The apartment in front of where you're living now is actually mine. I exchanged it with Raphael because the A/C in his apartment was broken. He cannot tolerate the summer heat. But now, the A/C has been repaired," he said, looking at Raphael, "Time to return to your apartment."

Raphael fake sobbed. "What do I do, Haelyn? We'll get separated. I'm moving away!" he exclaimed dramatically, grasping my hand.

"Yeah, away, like at the end of the floor, three apartments away," Castiel commented drily.

When Castiel wasn't looking, Raphael made a grimace at him while I tried to hide my laugh with a cough.

"Anyway, do you have anything to do tonight? We could order pizza and watch something to celebrate the reparation of the A/C," Raphael suggested.

"Sure, nowadays I only have paperwork at the office. I'm always free in the evening."

"Great! Being at the office all day must be boring. You deserve to chill a bit after."

"Yeah, can't wait till I move up from the paralegal position," I sighed.

"You're going to quit?" Raphael asked.

"No, I'll apply for another position in the law firm itself. I'm still not sure yet. I want to be a criminal investigator. If I don't get the position there,

I will leave. Or maybe not. I can apply for the criminal lawyer position as well. I need more time to think," I replied. I was a ball of confusion.

"You can start trying for a few positions in other law firms or organizations. An L.L.B and criminal justice degree plus your three years experience as a paralegal would look good enough on your resume," Castiel commented for the first time.

I leaned forward near his seat. "How do you know my degrees and how much time I worked at the law firm?" I asked, frowning with suspicion.

"Oh, uhm," he coughed, "E-Eliyah said so. You know she can't keep quiet at all," he stammered.

I leaned back in my seat. Well, figures. I also used to get all information about him from Eliyah. Not that I asked.

After finishing the pizza, we settled on the sofa in front of the television. We watched a random episode of Criminal Minds, meaning Raphael, Castiel, and I. Raphael had asked me to come to his apartment after he moved all his things back there, but Castiel invited himself in. I would have normally complained, but he was the one who ordered and paid for the pizza.

"Does watching crime shows help you a lot?" I asked curiously while focusing on the television.

"Ehh, well, sometimes it gives some clues or new insights, I guess," Raphael said.

"We don't need a scripted show to help us. Reality does not work that way," Castiel replied after. "Sure...," I drawled. "So, how far have you advanced with the Argan Gregore case? I can't hear any improvements despite submitting more clues," I inquired.

"Our main focus is the Doctor we heard from your phone recording. It could be a doctor of the Wellsworth Hospital or another hospital. But we are certain that it's someone from Wellsworth. We are watching all hospitals' activities closely," Raphael explained.

"And what about the names that I mentioned, I heard?" "The names Julian and Claris may be too broad of an idea to search. But we searched for a list of people with these names in all prisons and police stations. We are analyzing the list and eliminating them one by one," Raphael said.

"They may be searching for me right now. They already broke into my house twice. What if you guys use me as bait?" I asked, looking between them eagerly.

Both of them stared at me, then at each other, and again stared back at me.

"No," both voices echoed.

"Why not-"

"It's late now. We need to go to sleep," Castiel interrupted and stood up.

"Nah, I'll stay for some more minutes," I replied, leaning back.

"Get up," Castiel demanded and looked at Raphael, who stood up as well.

"Yes, you're right. It's quite late. Time just flew by."

I huffed and stood up as well. I said bye to Raphael and followed Castiel out.

When we arrived near our respective doors, Castiel turned to me and said, "Do not ever think about using yourself as bait again. That's a dangerous game you should not be playing. Good night."

I stared at the closed door. Well... a bummer. They had to admit, though, it was a nice idea.

I opened the door and went in. Judy seemed to be sleeping. I went to my room, changed into my pyjamas, and sat on my bed. I opened my laptop and clicked on the Argan Gregore Case Details document. I managed to recreate all reports and notes well. I should have mentioned this to everyone.

I went through the list of Doctors at Wellsworth Hospital I acquired some days back. I had to get more information on them to be able to suspect one of them. If I had to suspect someone right now, it was Dr. Martinez. He was the patient's doctor, always hated interviews, and already built assumptions.

I closed my laptop and laid down on my bed, getting comfortable. I closed my eyes and tried to get some sleep.

Thirty minutes later, I shot up in my bed in a sudden doubt. I got out of my bed and walked out of the apartment. I walked some meters ahead and knocked on Castiel's door.

But then I turned away. Maybe it's an insignificant doubt.

The door opened as I was thinking.

"Haelyn? What do you want?" I heard a puzzled voice.

I held up a finger. "Wait, I'm thinking."

I held my temples with both hands and gathered my thoughts. Turning around, I met Castiel's questioning eyes.

"So I have some suspicions..." I started, "or maybe not," I turned away again.

Castiel sighed and dragged me back to face him. "Just spit it out."

"Well, the other day, I was at the hospital and met someone. And while we were talking, his phone rang. That's why I could be suspecting him," I stated and continued, "When I looked at his phone, I saw the name Claris on it."

"What is his name?" Castiel asked, frowning.

"Dr. Alex Sullivan."

"Okay...I'll check into it. Go to sleep now. We'll talk about it tomorrow."

I headed back to my room, my head heavy with thoughts.

"Oh, you shouldn't be going into forests first. Such walks or runs do not always end nicely for some people," he advised.

Somehow, it no longer felt like advice now, more like a threat.

Castiel and Raphael had already left when I woke up the next morning. I went to work along with Judy as usual.

After I settled in my place, I stared blankly at the files in front of me. I grabbed my phone. Should I call Raphael? Did Castiel tell him? I really needed to know if my suspicions were true. Just then, I received a message from Eli.

Eli 10:30 am

I am at the Wellsworth Hospital for an interview with a victim. It happened to see Castiel and some of his friends around there. Do you know what he's up to?

Deciding that it was too long and complicated to explain over text, I told her no.

At least I knew what he was up to. I needed to get the information later. Or right now!

If only I had his num-

Wait. I grabbed my phone. I had used his phone to call mine before. Hehe, how convenient.

I called him. After a few seconds, he picked up.

"I'm working, Haelyn," were his first words.

...how did you know it was me?

'You had used my phone to call yours, remember?

"And you didn't delete it but instead saved it?"1

There was a pause.

"Well, I feel so special," I laughed.

"What. Do. You. Want?"

"Where are you?" I asked, getting back onto the subject.

"I know what you want to know. I'll tell you afterward," I heard, and he ended the call.

Ughh, so frustrating!

I returned my attention to my files. I needed to do it all faster, so I could go home early.

Five hours later, I gathered the stack of files and headed to Attorney Kim's office. With a loud bang, all files landed on his table.

I breathed heavily and wiped the sweat on my forehead. "Can I go now?" I asked, sounding desperate.

Attorney Kim looked at the files, seemingly impressed.

Then he looked at my hopeful eyes and pointed his finger to another stack of files.

I almost roared. You. Tasteless. Rancid. Kimchi.

"I will do those at home," I said patiently with a fake smile and gathered all the files that reached my chin.

Back in my room, I dropped the stack of files on the bed and ran outside again.

I almost slammed against Castiel's door. I took a deep intake of breath and calmed myself down. I tried to look as civilized as I could be and knocked. After two seconds, I ran out of civilized manners.

"Open, damn it!" I slammed my palm against his door.

The door opened within a few seconds, and before I could say anything, a hand grabbed mine and dragged me inside, shutting the door behind us.

"Be civilized, Carter. There are other people that live here."

"So, what did you do at the hospital?" I asked, leaning against the door. Then I looked down.

"Oh, Lord! Put a shirt on!" I exclaimed, turning around and almost kissing the door.

"If you had a bit more patience, maybe I would have had time to put one on. But no, someone had to act like a lunatic," a sarcastic reply came.

"Okay, sorry. Go," I gestured for him to move forward and put one on.

He walked away, but instead of putting a shirt on, he sat on the sofa. "This is my place. I don't need to put one on, actually," he said, smirking.

I rolled my eyes and sat down. "So start explaining. What did you do today?" I demanded while admiring the ceiling. It was plain white, but at least it was a view that kept me sane.

"I just spread some words around."

"What do you mean?" My head snapped back to his and returned to the ceiling.

"If Dr. Sullivan is the suspect, we must find some evidence. So some team members and I went to the hospital and spread the rumor that we would investigate all the doctors and other hospital staff. If there is more than one who is guilty, then they'll start showing it. They will start worrying and may meet up again. Some of us are keeping tabs on them, especially Dr. Sullivan."

"So, there is no investigation whatsoever?" I confirmed.

"None. Right now, it is not needed. It's just to push the necessary people out of their hiding."
"Okay," I said, standing up and looking at the door now, "Call me when my suspicions are confirmed true."

I started walking towards the door. Just then, Castiel's phone rang. My walking became slower.

"Where did you follow him to?" I heard him ask.

I made a swift turn and went to Castiel's side, gluing my ear to the other side of his phone. I heard something about a restaurant and waiting.

When the call ended, I asked, "What happened?"

"Dr. Sullivan is meeting up with someone at a restaurant."

"Can I go?" I asked with a cringe-pouting face.

"No," Castiel said with a grimace at my face, moving about to grab a shirt and put it on.

"Think about it. I could identify whoever will be meeting him," I attempted, trying to sound convincing.

Castiel paused for a while, considering it.

"And anyway, I'll be by your side. Safe," I added.

He sighed and nodded. I did a silent yippee and headed outside, waiting for him. In only one minute, Castiel joined me with a buttoned-up shirt, tie and suit. I nodded approvingly at him. He's got skills.

"Let's go," he said, heading to the elevator.

☆☆☆

Castiel navigated through the busy evening traffic of the London streets and reached the restaurant in thirty minutes.

Still, we got out of the car in the parking lot, and I spotted two familiar friends.

"Cooky! Shooky!" I yelled, waving wildly at them to get their attention. I didn't miss the facepalming Castiel did beside me, but I chose to ignore it as I went ahead.

"It's Lucio, Miss Carter," Shooky said when I approached him.

"And I'm Damian, not Cooky," Cooky said as he shivered with disgust at the beautiful name I gave him.

"And no one cares, Cooky and Shooky. So, what's the plan?" I asked, grinning.

Castiel joined us. "We should split into two groups and go in there. We will avoid the suspicion that way," Castiel said as he joined us.

"Okay," chorused Cooky and Shooky, who quickly turned around and left.

"We decided who will pair with who so fast," I nodded, impressed at our team skills.

"Don't be dumb. They don't want to be with you. Let's go fast. Dr. Sullivan is already inside."

I followed behind, rolling my eyes at him. As soon as I stepped in, I looked around. It seemed like a nice restaurant, giving a comfortable vibe.

I was going to walk beside Castiel when he stopped me. He took my hand and pushed me behind him. "Just stay behind me for now." He dragged me behind him to some people and talked about reservations. Damn it; we never made any reservations!

After a minute of discussion, Castiel led me to a table, and we sat beside each other near the window. The waiter approached us and handed us a menu.

Castiel quickly picked something and handed his menu back.

"And what would your girlfriend like, sir?"

"Oh, I'm not-"

I got cut off by Castiel, who picked my menu. He scanned the menu, picked a random item, and sent the waiter away.

"You could have let me decide," I glared at him.

We are not here to eat.

"Yes, but the food is food. It's as important," I said.

"My job first. Sullivan is sitting with a man two tables behind, to your left," Castiel replied.

Curious, I turned around to look at him when Castiel lifted his arm, wrapping it around my shoulders, and pushed my face to his chest.

"Pff, what are you doing?" I tried to ask as my face crashed against his chest. "Let me go!" I fumed, trying to push him.

"Stop," he said firmly. I dropped my hands as I leaned my head on his shoulder instead.

"What are you trying to do?" I whispered harshly.

"I should be the one asking you this. Those men could be those who are trying to kill you. Are you that stupid to show your face and expose yourself and me?"

"Oh, I didn't realize. Curiosity got the best of me. But can you let go of me?"

"No, we are posing as a couple right now. I can't risk you blowing our cover."

"I never got informed of having to act as a couple."

It's an on-the-spot decision.

"But I need to see..." I drawled and got an idea. I took my phone out of my purse.

I grinned. "Since we are a lovey-dovey couple of a date, let's take a selfie," I declared.

I wrapped my arms around Castiel's shoulder, drawing him closer. I think I almost choked him. Ha, revenge is so sweet!

I smiled and took the selfie. I analyzed the photo. How did he look good even while being expressionless?

I zoomed in on the other people I got in the photo. Geez, I wasn't able to get the right people.

"Another one," I sighed.

I positioned my phone a bit farther away to include those behind us. As I was about to click, I saw another person approaching Dr. Sullivan's table. My phone slipped out of my hand and fell on my lap. I froze.

"What? What is it?" Castiel asked carefully.

Ignoring his earlier words, I turned around and looked at Dr. Sullivan's table to ensure I saw correctly. Castiel swiftly turned me back again.

"What, Haelyn?" Castiel asked irritatedly.

"I'm not sure if I saw clearly, but the person that just joined the table greatly resembles Argus, Argan Gregore's brother," I said softly, frowning.

"Are you sure?"

"I just said I'm not! I only met him once. Though I did think I saw him again, I ignored my doubts because right now, he is supposed to be in Italy," I explained.

"We'll confirm it later then. Let me take the photo again."

While Castiel took some photos, my thoughts kept running over and over. I looked at Castiel.

"Don't look at me. You're right in their front sight. They'll notice you."

I turned to the window, looking outside. "But it does not make sense! What would he be doing with Dr. Sullivan, out of all people, if that's him? We suspect these people of the murder of his brother! Or are we wrong?" I started saying.

Soon, the waiter came with the food. I remained quiet and waited for him to leave.

I nudged Castiel with my elbow. "What do you think?"

"There may be things we are unaware of, but I am not wrong; I know," he said confidently. Ughh, that ego of his! I hoped one day I could prove him wrong.

"What if I walk up to them and say hi?" I asked.

"No, you definitely won't do anything as such when I'm around. Let them be. Lucio and Damian will stay here a bit longer. Continue eating, and then we leave," Castiel said.

I sighed. After eating, Castiel paid and made us leave through the backdoor instead of the front one. He said I could get easily noticed if I passed before them.

We walked back to the car and waited for Cooky and Shooky.

"That was a very boring undercover mission," I commented.

"Only because you were there. I can't risk exposing you to them. I mean, I'll get in trouble with the organization," Castiel remarked.

"Whatever, don't blame me for your lack of strategies and skills," I said, crossing my arms. "You must have played many roles while doing an undercover operation, right?" I asked curiously.

"Hmm, what about it?"

"How many times have you played a couple with others? I'm just curious, don't misunderstand," I said.

I looked at Castiel out of the corner of my eyes. He was smirking.

So?

He shrugged.

"Is that a no? Or you don't remember?"

He shrugged again.

Persisting would only make me look desperate. So I didn't say anything afterward and instead continued looking outside, waiting for Cooky and Shooky.

☆☆☆

It was my day off. Finally.

I decided to go to a new cafe that opened a week ago. The cafes were my second home. It was my field of expertise. I visited almost all the cafes in London, close or far, it didn't matter.

This one was a bit far, so I took the bus alone. I told Judy to tag along afterward because I needed some time alone.

The bus ride was almost an hour long. I arrived at the cafe at lunchtime. Who goes to a cafe for lunch? Yup, that's me.

I entered the cafe. There were very few people. Unlike others, my free day was usually on Monday. So wherever I went during my free days, it was always less crowded.

I sat down, looking at the large menu charts on the wall. Hmm, how much should I eat there and how much should I take home? I should buy a cake for Eli as well. But then Raphael would maybe like one too. He bought a cheesecake for me some days ago. And Castiel...he likes cupcakes. Should I-

"Haelyn Carter?" I heard a surprised voice.

My train of thought got interrupted. I looked up from my seat.

Argus.

Before I could say anything, he spoke up. "I returned from Italy two days ago. I had to take care of an emergency, so I was gone for a while."

"Sure...," I drawled, not knowing what to say.

Argus looked around hesitantly and spoke again. "I wanted to know about my brother. I wanted to contact you before, but I lost the contact card you gave me."

"Sure," I nodded and bit my lip, "you can sit down." I gestured to the seat in front of me.

"I am a bit uncomfortable publicly talking about my brother's death. I'm staying in the apartment right across this cafe," he said, pointing to the building across the road. "I would appreciate it if we could talk there. For only a few minutes," he added.

"Okay, sure. Lead the way," I said, standing up.

Argus breathed in relief and gave me a polite smile. We left the cafe, and I followed him to his apartment on the third floor.

He opened the door and gestured for me to step in. He kicked the door shut and told me to sit on the chair nearby. "Wait here. I'll bring a glass of water for you," he said.

I nodded and sat down, looking around. It seemed empty. I heard Argus speaking. Oh, he must be speaking on the phone.

I waited and waited. I was about to turn around and check when I felt something sharp pressing against my neck.

"Don't move," I heard a calm voice.

"What are you doing?" I asked in a harsh startled tone as I felt ropes sliding around my waist, pressing me against the chair. Both of my hands were dragged behind, tightened together by the rope. I tried to move and kicked the chair with my free legs. Wrong move.

The next thing I knew was my legs being tied to the chair. This couldn't be happening! This was so fucked up!

I opened my mouth to speak again when I saw the knife near my face. I closed my mouth.

I looked up to meet Argus' non-smiling and blank face, analyzing my state.

Seeing that it was all good, he went to the door and locked it.

"What do you want from me, Argus?" I said with a sigh after minutes of silence. I turned to Argus, sitting on the sofa beside me, playing with a knife. He continued prolonging the silence.

"Everything you said to me was a lie, right?" I asked as peacefully as I could while eyeing the knife wearily.

He again remained silent.

"Look, I can help you if you have been threatened into-"

"Yes."

"Huh, yes, what?" I asked, startled.

"Yes, I lied about everything. I was not threatened with doing this. And I feel sorry for you, but you got into this mess by playing detective. I'd advise you to stop now."

I rolled my eyes. He was right. But considering my situation, it was late now.

"Was Argan being your brother a lie too?" I asked, ignoring what he said.

He stared at me. He must have been thinking about whether he should reveal everything or not.

"You are already holding me, hostage right now," I added, gesturing to my hands which I could barely move.

"He was my brother," Argus finally said and turned away.

"And? How is that linked to you doing all this?" I asked encouragingly.

"I made a deal for some people to get rid of him."

"Oh ok- Wait, what?" I asked, perplexed.

"Remember what he was in prison for?"

"It was an assault case. He was charged by his girlfriend. How is that related?" I asked again, even more confused.

"He had been abusing his girlfriend both emotionally and physically for more than two years and blackmailed her into remaining silent. But she was not the only one suffering from such abuse. My brother always had violent tendencies. After my parents' death, he became more violent and used to take out all his rage on me," he said as he clenched his jaw. He must have been reliving some memories. Then he continued. "As I approached my eighteenth birthday, I wanted to escape from my home. But my brother warned me not to do so or else he'll find me...and kill me. So I secretly informed the police about him. One day, when he beat up his girlfriend, the police arrived and took him away. This was freedom for me. I took all that I could and left for Italy."

"Oh, so this part was true," I mumbled.

He continued, "Some months prior to his 'disappearance,' he had passed a message to me through some gang member with whom he had contacts for drugs. He said that I better be at home when he would be released, or else he would hunt me down. I can't have my past repeating, so I made sure he'll be gone forever this time."

"I sympathize with you, but you should not have taken the illegal way to get rid of your problem. I'm sure the police would have helped you. But what deal did you make? With whom? Like, did you just appoint someone to kill him? After all this, why did you file a case for his disappearance?"

"I can't tell you anything beyond what I just said. They won't spare you if you get to know more than needed."

Just then, I heard a knock on the door. I shifted my eyes to the door with hope. But seeing that Argus lazily walked over to the door, it seemed that he was expecting someone.

I held my breath as I stared at the door. Argus unlocked the door, and four men entered. Argus swiftly closed the door and locked it. I couldn't see their faces because they all had caps on, with their heads down, to not bring attention to them as they entered. But I could guess who they were. The first man removed his cap and smiled at me. The same smile he gave me when we first met a few days ago. A deceptive one.

"We meet again, Haelyn Carter," he said with a warmth that made me freeze. I could not show him that I was scared. I masked my feelings behind a blank expression.

He only chuckled and grabbed a nearby chair, pulling it and placing it in front of me. He sat down and stared at me.

His henchmen, including Argus, stood behind him silently. I recognized one of the men, who I supposed was Julian.

Then I looked at Dr. Sullivan, who was still looking at me with a smile, but his eyes were cold and calculating.

"Hi, Dr. Gulliver- Oops, I mean Sullivan. What brings you here?" I asked, returning his fake smile.

"Your plays won't work here, Haelyn," he smirked. "And it seems yours work everywhere," I retorted with a scoff.

"Look at your state. You are in no position to speak like that," he said dryly. He's got the point.

"It seems that what you need is for me to talk. And that's not something in your power," I said sharply.

Dr. Sullivan chuckled and turned to Argus, reaching for the knife. And Argus dutifully gave him the knife while looking down.

"Are you happy, Argus? I mean, while trying to get rid of a monster of your past, you now have to serve another one," I sneered, looking Dr. Sullivan straight in the eyes. Argus, however, did not look at me or say one word.

"He agreed to the deal, sweetie. He has to suck it up," Dr. Sullivan laughed.

"And is this what I am here for? Another deal you're trying to make?" I smirked.

"I hope for your own good that it's a deal you'll agree to, or the other choice is a contract of death," he commented in turn.

"Wow, I thought you were a doctor. Aren't you supposed to save lives instead of killing?" I mused. I tried to sound as mocking as I could with only my head while the rest of my body started feeling stiff. "We are not here to talk about me. I saw that you like investigating and doing interviews a lot. Now, it is my turn to interview you, and you better talk," Dr. Sullivan said while twisting the knife in his hand.

"What did you see that night? I know you followed me," I heard the man I recognized as Julian ask.

So, he was the one pretending to be a hospital employee.

I stared at him. Should I refuse to answer? If I refuse, then this knife will meet me soon. Lying is a better solution.

"I didn't get to the building. I only entered the woods and got lost."

"Don't kid with me. How did you know there was a building then?" Julian retaliated.

I lowered my head, trying to sound as truthful and serious as possible.

"I fell somewhere in the woods. A stranger was passing by in a hurry. I thought he was the one I followed, but he helped me up and told me to run. He said he discovered a place he shouldn't have. So I kept running until I came out of the woods," I ended my act with a heavy sigh.

"If you knew it had nothing to do with you, why did you not return to your apartment?" he asked again, scrutinizing my reaction.

"I was injured, so I spent a night at the hospital. The next day, my apartment was in total disorder. I didn't feel safe, so I left and stayed with a friend. It's logical. From what I heard, my apartment was broken into again a few days after. It encouraged me even more not to come back." "I don't care about that. If it was not you, then prove it. Who was the stranger?" Dr. Sullivan snapped.

"How would I know his identity? It was at night, and he was wearing a hoodie. Half of his face was already hidden," I exclaimed incredulously.

"And I didn't find anything, to begin with. I know nothing about where, how, or when Argan Gregore died. You all stole all files I had about him, so you must know what I found out didn't even scratch the surface of the truth. And I lost the case a day after. It's been weeks, and I did nothing related to that case. So why are you suspecting me?" I ranted at them, sounding offended. Mentally, I grinned and patted myself on the shoulder. Good acting. Keep it up!

They were all analyzing me, trying to see if I was lying. Half of what I said was true, though.

I maintained a poker face and waited for them to say something.

Dr. Sullivan leaned back in his chair and crossed his arms. Was he showing off his privilege of having the freedom of movement compared to my situation? I couldn't even lean back comfortably in this chair.

"Let's pretend what you said is true. It is still obvious you are hiding something," Dr. Sullivan concluded.

"There is no need to pretend when I am telling the truth! You abducted the wrong person, I'm telling you. I didn't know shit about you guys until you all had to go ahead, wrecking my place and now abducting me. Meanwhile, other people are investigating and searching for you right now. I was miles away from the actual truth, but who knows, the actual investigators may be only a footstep away."

Right in time, I heard the doorbell ring, and a knock followed. Everyone glanced at each other, stunned. They were not expecting anyone else.

"Who is it?" Dr. Sullivan yelled, frustrated at the unexpected guest interrupting.

"Pizza delivery!" I heard a cheerful voice answer.

Aww, the two words that always brought a smile to my face. Even the voice seemed familiar.

We all looked at Argus. He shook his head, signaling that he didn't order.

"Go away! We didn't order!" Julian yelled back in turn.

There was silence. Then a louder knock followed. I would have jumped with surprise if it wasn't for the ropes holding me in place.

"I didn't come all this way for the pizza to be returned. I demand you take it and pay for it. I have had enough of pranks!"

I was going to yell, "I'll take it!" when I was stopped by a hand clamped firmly over my mouth.

Some silent planning went on as the ropes wrapped around me were cut. I was going to release a big breath and yell for freedom, but the men gathered around me, taking me by my hands and legs to the farthest room. They made me sit on the bed, tying my hands only. Dr. Sullivan held a knife near my throat, warning me not to utter a word.

"Claris, go deal with that annoying boy and return when he leaves," Dr. Sullivan ordered one of the guys, who nodded and left to open the door.

We remained in an awkward silence waiting for them to talk and for Claris to return. But he didn't. And we couldn't hear anything. The room must have been too far away.

"I think someone else should go and see what our friend Claris is up to. I think he is eating the whole pizza himself," I chimed in lowly and stopped when the knife came closer.

"Argus, go take a look. I wonder what is taking so long," Julian said.

Argus went out. We waited. He didn't come back.

"I'm telling you, you three will regret it. They are probably finishing the pizza right now," I said, shaking my head with disappointment. I tried my best not to laugh, considering the situation.

The other man stepped forward and headed to the door, seemingly frustrated. He was met with a gun pointed at his head as he opened it. He became a frozen statue.

Castiel took advantage of his surprise, instantly twisting his hands around and handcuffing him. He pushed him behind, passing him to other agents who led him out. I heard some distant shouts.

Castiel slowly stepped inside, raising his hand, pointing the gun at me or Dr. Sullivan, who swiftly positioned himself right behind me, with the knife pressing against my neck. I held my breath.

"I told you not to follow him anywhere. Now, look what your stupidity got yourself into," Castiel remarked. He can nag in the middle of any situation. I wanted to say anything to retaliate, but the knife prevented me from even breathing. But he was partly right. I thought back to our earlier conversation.

flashback

I was sitting in a board meeting with five special agents. I felt like one as well.

"Are you sure you can do this?" Cooky confirmed for the hundredth time. I nodded again and avoided the gaze of Castiel, who had been glaring at me for the past ten minutes.

He was completely opposed to using me as bait, saying that I was the type that would lead me into an even more dangerous situation. That was the reason I approached the others about this idea instead of suggesting it to him.

"Here," Cooky said, handing me a black watch.

"Is this a gift because of my awesome plan?" I asked as I put it around my wrist, admiring it.

Raphael tried to stifle a laugh. I glared at him. "What's funny?"

"This watch is a voice recorder. It has an embedded mic on both sides. For it to start recording, push the small switch on the left," he said. "Oh, and you have to return it after. It's not a gift," he laughed. I rolled my eyes at him.

"Back to the plan. You have to be cautious and not overdo it," Cooky warned.

"Do not be nervous. Do not look around for us. You should show that you are unaware he has returned from Italy. Do not ask questions out of the list we have given you. And for God's sake, do not go anywhere alone with him, places where there is no one that is, if you are too stupid to understand," Castiel explained. I ignored him, concentrating instead on the watch they gave me. I couldn't wait until I could test it.

"I'll wait at the cafe opposite the building where you said he is currently living. He may spot me more easily that way, and it would look more natural," I said, and everyone agreed.

"And do not leave the cafe with him. If he goes in, talk there itself. If they were trying to abduct you, once they get the opportunity again, they'd seize it," Castiel said again. I huffed and nodded.

end of flashback

As I stared at him, I knew I would not get away with it. He has to save me before Dr. Sullivan's knife gets to me first. I would listen to him all my life if I were alive after this.

I was having difficulty breathing with a sharp knife pressed against my throat. And Castiel stood by the door, his gun now trained on Julian's head, who also happened to have a gun with him.

I heard some struggling and fighting from outside. I wondered how many men came for this raid. After a few seconds, Raphael also arrived dressed in a pizza delivery worker's clothes. I was slightly disappointed that it was only an act. I was in the mood for a real pizza.

I closed my eyes and told myself to come back to my senses. I could die right now. The man holding the knife to my throat was a doctor. He's got the skills for a precise cut and kill.

Seeing Raphael coming in as well, Dr. Sullivan stepped back, wary. He gestured to the knife in his hand as a warning. Raphael pointed his gun at Dr. Sullivan in response. What more will they do now? A staring competition?

"Get out of the room, and we won't kill her," Dr. Sullivan warned.

"No, can do that," Castiel replied right away. Wow, he must really hate me.

The knife pressed harder at the side of my neck. I gasped as I felt a slight sting. From Castiel and Raphael's reactions, I deduced that he must have done this to show that his threat was real.

If I did not do anything, Dr. Sullivan and his sidekick would be able to run away. I looked at Julian, who was two meters away from Dr. Sullivan and me. I cast a glance downward at the knife. If I tried to move away in any direction, the knife would definitely come in contact with the neck again, with full damage.

I looked at Castiel, who was pointing a gun at Julian. He gave me a side glance. He looked down and nodded at me. I gave him a puzzled look. What did he want to say? I tried to look down, but the knife stopped me.

Okay, I got it. I took a deep breath and counted.

One...
Two...
Three!

I stomped hard on Dr. Sullivan's foot. Considering that I was wearing heels, it must have hurt. Hissing in surprise, he looked out and moved his hand away from my throat. Seizing the opportunity, I grabbed the hand holding the knife and turned it around as I got out of his reach.

It must have hurt as I twisted his hand. He dropped the knife, and I kicked it sideways. Seeing what was going on, Julian's gun turned towards me. I copied Dr. Sullivan's earlier move, positioning myself behind him, and kicked him in Julian's direction.

Julian's gun went up as he fell, a gunshot resonating in the building.

Raphael and Castiel rushed into action. The brave me ran out of the room.

I was going to run out of the apartment but then decided against it. There could be a possibility of one of them running away. They may need me, my delusional self-thought.

I peeked into the room again to see Castiel raining blows on Dr. Sullivan. Ha! Yes! Served him right. Make mashed potatoes out of him!

Being of a bigger build and having lots of training, Castiel easily empowered Dr. Sullivan. It was obvious that this was not his field of expertise. However, Julian was more skilled at fighting. Raphael had kicked his gun aside when he fell. He couldn't reach for it as he was busy defending himself from Raphael's punches. He held himself well at first when he managed to block Raphael's punches. But his fighting skills were more unstable compared to Raphael's calculated moves. Raphael had the upper hand because of professional training. I kept analyzing their actions, acting as a commentator in my head.

As Julian continued resisting, I saw his furrowed eyebrows. He knew he wouldn't be able to last. Julian rushed to the door, swinging a fist at Raphael, temporarily holding him back. Exactly where I was standing.

I stood there in case they needed me, but my fighting skills worsened. I sucked at fighting, but playing tricks were my fort.

I hurried against the wall to let Julian run past without harming me. Then, as he sprinted by, I stretched one foot out. And boom, he fell hard on the floor. I moved away in case he got up to attack me. Another agent came with handcuffs. Raphael prevented Julian from standing up while the agent put the handcuffs on him. I took the other handcuffs to Castiel, who was handling a half-conscious, completely battered, Dr. Sullivan.

"Don't you think you kinda overdid it?" I commented, cringing at Castiel's victim's face.

"I'll take him," said the other agent, entering and dragging Dr. Sullivan mercilessly out of the room.

My eyes followed them and returned to Castiel. "So...admit it. I did a great job," I grinned at him expectantly.

"Very few things can make me worry, but congrats, your stupidity is one of them," he finally said, pursing his lips with disapproval.

"And very few things can affect me, but pity, your nasty remarks ain't one of them," I retorted, rolling my eyes.1

He sighed and looked at me intensely. He raised one hand, approaching my face. I was about to speak again when his hand grabbed my face, squeezing my cheeks.

"Wbht urr yah dwing?" I sputtered.

He pushed my face aside, analyzing my neck. He let go of my face and touched my neck instead. It stung again.

Castiel raised his hand in front of me again. "This is the result of your great job," he said, showing me the blood on his fingers.

"AND five men arrested," I added proudly.

"You are too ambitious," Castiel said, shaking his head, going out.

"I learned from the best," I piped in with a smile, following him.

☆☆☆

"Yikes, that's so frikitty tickitty bad. I'm telling you, it stings! Stop!" I exclaimed, trying to push Castiel away, as I sat on the counter in his kitchen.

His arm rounded around my neck even harder, preventing me from moving as he cleaned the slight 'scratch' that I got.

He dragged me into his apartment after seeing my 'bad' first aid method. It was simply a light cut, so I thought putting multiple band-aids to cover it would do the job. But apparently, it didn't.

"Stop kicking your legs," he instructed while I continued resisting. He was too slow. It seemed that he enjoyed seeing me in pain. He stood nearer, capturing my legs between his to prevent me from moving.

I forgot how to breathe.

"C-can you put your face away? You're in my breathing space!" I stammered.

He didn't reply, concentrating hard on the trivial task. I closed my eyes and prayed that he finish soon. After a few more seconds, he moved his hand away.

"There. That's how it's done," he said. I placed my hand on my neck, feeling it completely covered. I opened my eyes and was met with Castiel's face only two inches away from mine. I immediately moved away due to the proximity.

"Yeah, okay. Thanks. Move away," I blurted, with a flustered face.

"Ooh, what's going on?" I heard a voice from outside the kitchen. I took a look and spotted Raphael entering.

"Nothing," Castiel and I echoed.

Raphael stood still, glancing between us back and forth as if trying to figure out something. Then, he shrugged. "Move, then. You're blocking my way to the fridge."

Castiel and I gave him a weird look. Castiel moved his legs to free mine as I jumped off the counter. "It's my fridge, though," he mumbled.

"Yes, I never said it was mine," Raphael countered nonchalantly. The shameless guy walked to the fridge, opened it, and examined what treasures lay inside. Castiel shook his head with a sigh and got out of the kitchen. Seeing that he was gone, I also joined Raphael, taking a peek inside. Hmm, some bottles of water, veggies, fruits...boring.

I looked in the freezer. Then I looked at Raphael, who returned my grin. We fist-bumped and took out the ice cream. Both of us took a bowl each and headed to the living room, lying on the sofa and making ourselves comfortable as Raphael turned on the TV.

Castiel joined us after a few minutes. I noticed that he had changed into more comfortable clothes. He didn't join us. Instead, he only stood with some expression that I couldn't figure out. I felt like he was going to cry.

With a mouthful of ice cream, I said, "You should thank me. I left some for you. Raph was going to take everything, but I stopped him."

He pursed his lips, went to the kitchen, and returned with the box of ice cream. I had never seen such a sad look on his face before. I slapped his back in comfort.

"It's okay; you'll get a better one next time," I offered.

His glare returned, and I quickly looked back to the TV.

We sat in silence for a while. Then I turned to Raphael. "By the way, are you okay? You took quite a punch earlier," I remarked, seeing his swollen cheek and red knuckles.

"It's not bad compared to more dangerous situations we went through before. The swelling will go away in time," he shrugged.

"Okay. But if you need some fix-up or it's hurting, you can ask Castiel. He is good at it," I said, nodding at Castiel.

Raphael raised an eyebrow at Castiel, who shook his head firmly.

"He is," I insisted, "Even back in school, he was good at it. He had once bandaged my head due to an injury I received...from himself. I got hit by his ball," I frowned at the memory.

"It was an accident," Castiel mumbled with a scowl. "Aw, how cute," Raphael cooed at us. "Tell me more," he said, putting one leg over the other, his hands resting on his knees, leaning forward for gossip.

I stared at him. Castiel stared at him. He stared at us. Castiel stood up. "I have to make a call," he said and walked away.

Raphael's eyes followed him, then returned to me expectantly. I shrugged. He rushed to my side.

"So, how close are you both? I was itching to ask that, but I was afraid of another punch. I've never heard him talk to you during the few years I've known him, but you always came up when he talked about high school memories. So?" he nudged me.

"We were...," I trailed off, searching for an appropriate word to define our relationship, "uhm, classmates," I finished.

"Obviously, but how close were you both?" Raphael scoffed.

"We were not," I replied.

"So...you weren't friends?" he confirmed. I nodded.

"So you were enemies?"

I nodded again.

"You hate him?"

"Well...yeah, or maybe not. He just pisses me off sometimes. But he's okay on rare occasions. I can talk with him like civilized people one second and try to murder him the next second," I attempted to explain.

"So, you can admit he's likable for at least a second?" Raphael said, grinning.

"What do you mean? And stop smiling like that," I asked, annoyed. He had that look, the one where he was constructing a scheme in his head.

"Are you both quite finished? We need to head back to the headquarters for the interrogation of the suspects," I heard and turned back to see a well-dressed Castiel walking towards the door. Oh, right, we were in his apartment.

"I'll come as well!" I exclaimed, shooting off my seat. Castiel had the 'not again' look on his face. "Don't you have work or other things to do?" he asked with hope.

"I refuse to work on another day off. Wait for me. I'll change and come back in one minute!"

"Same!" Raphael said, getting up as he followed me out of Castiel's apartment.

I rushed to Judy's apartment. She was lying on the sofa with a book. She looked surprised to see me. "Forgot to inform you I'll be returning earlier. But the more free time for you. I'm going to...hang out with Castiel," I said, excusing myself as I rushed into my room.

Seeing as those agents are always dressed in suits, I searched for black pants and the white blouse I usually wore to work. This would match them. I nodded at myself in the mirror.

In one minute, I was ready to go. I walked out of the apartment without looking at Judy again.

Castiel looked surprised to see me ready in one minute. "What?" I demanded, standing by his side.

"I thought you'd take as much time as Raphael does," he said, shaking his head.

"What do you mean?" I asked, confused.

"Let's wait," he chuckled.

Thirty minutes later, Raphael came out of his apartment. I stared blankly at him, crossing my arms.

He grinned at us, ignoring the look I was giving him. He did a twirl and brushed his hand through his blond curls. "How do I look?" he asked.

"Like trash," I said, withholding all expressions from my face.

"Right," Castiel pursed his lips, hiding a smile. "Let's go."

We went forward, ignoring the dramatic gasp behind us.

☆ ☆☆

I walked into the room, separated by the interrogation room with glass. I saw Mr. Ford already seated, discussing something with Shooky.

He smiled as I walked in with his two agents. He stood up and approached us.

"Good job capturing these goons," he expressed, nodding at the two agents. Then he turned to me,

"And thank you as well. Without you, we wouldn't have been able to get them all together so soon."

"It's my dut- I mean, it's my pleasure, sir," I beamed.

He nodded and told us, "The interrogation session is over for now. You should all head to the meeting room where the others are. I'll join you in a while."

I sighed and gave Mr. Ford a polite smile. As I turned around and headed to the meeting room with Castiel and Raphael, I nudged Raphael harshly with my elbow. He yelped, making me smile with satisfaction. "You made us miss it," I huffed.

Raphael huffed back and pinched my arm.

I gaped at his guts.

"You gutter rat!" I slapped the back of his head.

He pulled out his tongue at me and flicked my head.

I felt the temperature rise on my face. This was war.

I swung my leg around for a kick. I missed it due to Raphael's fast reflexes. I swung my hand, and I missed again. Raphael was smirking by then, making me more tempted to slap off that expression. Show off.

I ran to him, but he kept dodging my moves, running even farther. I knew I needed serious practice compared to a professional agent. I ran after him, but he only laughed and sped up around the corner. He was more familiar with the headquarters. I couldn't keep up.

Turning around to face the indifferent Castiel, who was walking at his normal pace, I ran up to him or behind him, to be more specific.

I jumped on his back.

"After that, man! Quick!"

Castiel ran as slow as a turtle or didn't want to give me a first-class piggyback ride.

"We've lost the man. I didn't pay you for this slow ride! Can't you go faster?" I sighed with exasperation. "I wish I could, but you w-"

"Don't you dare insult my weight," I hissed, my hands going around his neck as a warning?

He remained silent. Good choice.

He guided us to a meeting room, which I assumed Raphael already ran into. I got off my ride and followed him in. Raphael sat beside Cooky, his head facing down to hide his smile.

I smiled as well, walking around to sit right in front of him. When he looked up, I made the throat-slitting gesture with a serious face and kicked his legs from under the table. I ignored his pained expression and looked at the others.

"So, what are we discussing? Did they reveal anything important?" I asked.

"Yes and no. They did answer some questions but refused to answer the deeper questions," one of the interrogators, Ferdinand, said.

"Firstly, what did they plead guilty to?" I asked, readying my other questions mentally.

"Abducting and murdering Argan Gregore since that was the only case we have them in detention. The recording of your conversation does not hint at further cases. All men said they did it because Argus made a deal with them. Dr. Sullivan claimed he was threatened by the gang in doing it," Ferdinand summarised.

"Hmm, that sounds like a load of crap," Raphael mused, raising an eyebrow.

"Right. That abandoned building had more than one dead body. So it's not only because of Argus' deal. And Dr. Sullivan definitely was not threatened. He seemed to have taken the role of the leader among them," I noted.

"But wait, why did Argus file a case against the hospital if he was the one behind his brother's disappearance?" I asked, frowning. It didn't make sense.

"He was afraid that if an investigation were to be carried out, he would be suspected since there is enough proof of animosity between the brothers and his engagement in gangs. He thought the case would be dropped easily soon after the death of his brother was discovered. The result right now is half true. The case has been dropped today, but with him being the suspect," Ferdinand said, shrugging.

I had a little sympathy for him because of his past. However, the past could be used as an excuse for future actions. He chose the wrong path.

"What type of gangs was Argus involved in?" Castiel asked.

"When I interrogated him, his explanations were vague. He said that he did make friends from gangs back in Italy. So the deal must have been done there.

It was perhaps not some small gangs, though, since they had contacts here to get it done, I believe through the suspects we just arrested. Our suspects here do not seem to have enough power or reason to commit multiple murders. Someone with more influence must have instructed them on what to do," Ferdinand expressed.

Hmm, in the end, Dr. Sullivan and company were no big players in the game.

"But even so, it's not a random killing that they are doing, I presume," I said, looking at the others for confirmation. What reason could there exist for random murders? There was no pattern following each case as well. None of the victims were related. Even the people committing the murders were not related.

"Until we do further interrogations, we can't be certain of our theories," Shooky inserted.

"But we did get word from other teams, even outside England, of similar operations. Small groups of people are put together to carry out those crimes, so even if arrested, there won't be a risk of the main group pulling the strings. This increases the power of the group without any major loss or secrets spilling," Raphael said.

"When I had overheard them at the warehouse, they did mention a boss," I commented.

"I asked about it to everyone. They said they had never met that boss they mentioned before. If that 'boss' does not want to risk exposure, then they may be telling the truth," Ferdinand replied.

"We'll get more answers if we know with whom Argus made the deal in Italy," Raphael said, sighing as he crossed his arms in thought.

Right then, a knock interrupted the discussion, followed by the entrance of Mr. Ford.

He didn't sit down. Instead, he marched towards the middle as our attention span on him.

"I just had a few discussions, and I'll reveal some details with you all tomorrow. For now, I have news for you," he said. Everyone's attention perked up.

"You all will be going to Italy tomorrow evening, of course, with the exception of Miss Carter here. Come back in the morning for a brief over. For now, nothing additional has to be discussed." Oh...that was nice.

Everyone nodded. They must be used to such random demands of going here and there since they did not look surprised. We all stood up, said our greetings, and started heading out.

The ride back was a bit quieter. I believed it was because the exhaustion was catching upon us. Even Raphael did not talk much.

Raphael turned to me and hugged me as we reached our respective doors. Castiel rolled his eyes at him.

"I'll miss you sooo much!" he fake cried.

I rolled my eyes and patted his back. A bit harshly.

"Ouch. Thanks for love," he said, letting go, glaring at me.

"Anytime," I grinned.

"Anyway, don't forget to see us before we leave. It may take weeks before we will return back," Raphael said, returning to his normal self.

"Hmm, I'm not sure. I am returning to my apartment tonight since those who were hunting me are now caught, and tomorrow I got work. I'll see if I could pop by," I said, shrugging.

"I better get a goodbye from you," Raphael said firmly, then walked to his apartment.

My gaze switched from him back to Castiel. I raised an eyebrow at him. He raised an eyebrow back at me. "Later," I said with a shrug and entered Judy's apartment.

Our goodbyes were as awkward as our hellos. What should I have said? Good riddance?

☆☆☆

I put the box with my things in the living room, back at my apartment. I was surprised that my apartment was clean and back to its original state. I remembered clearly that I left it in disorder. Just then, I heard a thing notifying me of a message. I took out my phone. It was a text from my Dad. A smile instantly formed on my face.

Dad 10:05

You must have already arrived back at your place. I had come back a few days after the second break-in to see if any of those goons were still around. I also fixed a camera at your door. And I didn't want you to come back to such a mess, so I cleaned it up. I'm quite busy these days so I'll visit you later. Love you.

I chuckled to myself and analyzed my apartment. It looked quite polished and shiny. My Dad was such a clean freak, not that I ever complained. I should be the one to visit him, I thought. Due to his hectic schedule, it was hard for him to travel back and forth from Cambridge to London.

I sent him a message back, thanking him for everything. I went into my office, putting my bag on the table. It was not an office, but I liked to call it so. When I bought the apartment, it had two rooms, so I converted one into an office, half of which was filled with bookshelves. I checked around to make sure all my files were there. I needed to start locking it every day now.

I looked at the time. 10:15. I usually sleep later, but today's incidents made me a bit tired. I decided to go to sleep. It would do me some good before going back to normal tomorrow.

☆☆☆

"Here, a cappuccino for you," I said, putting it on Eliyah's desk.

"Where were you yesterday?" Eli shot at me as soon as I sat down.

"We are at work right now," I commented.

"Have you looked at the time? There are still five minutes till work officially starts. Spill," Eliyah said drily.

I looked left and right and back to Eliyah. "First, bring your chair next to mine," I whispered.

Eliyah eagerly jumped onto my side with the cappuccino.

I scanned my surroundings again and then spilled everything that happened yesterday, leaving out most of the case's details. I tried to sum it up as best as I could.

I took a deep breath after finishing. Eliyah remained silent for a while, and her gaze even fell on my neck to get a glimpse of the injury.

"So...you're telling me you jumped into the lion's den willingly, asking to get killed?" Eliyah gave me her interpretation of the matter.

"I used myself as bait to capture all criminals at once," I rephrased her sentence and remarked, "And they are no lions, more like petty and annoying hyenas."

"You act too carelessly. Thank God Castiel, and his team arrived at the right moment. He saved your life once more," Eliyah sighed, shaking her head.

"Pfft, you always hold him in too high esteem," I scoffed, "Anyways, you up for a sleepover today?"

"Duh! It's been a while since we spent time together outside work. You were always with Castiel," Eli smirked.

"Correction," I held out one finger, "I was with my new friend, Raphael. But Castiel always tagged along. You should meet him one day. Raphael is like the male version of you," I said with a chuckle.

"If I could please interrupt your conversation, ladies," I heard an approaching voice.

Both Eliyah and I turned around to see Mr. Wallace, one of the lawyers we work under.

"Oh shit! I forgot that I need to go to court with him," Eliyah whispered and groaned.

"There are some files you need to take from Attorney Kim. Fetch them and wait by my car. Meanwhile, I'll take care of a pressing matter and come," Mr. Wallace said as he passed by quickly toward his office.

Eliyah looked at him, hurrying away, and stood up with a sigh.

"Seems like we have to reschedule our conversation to tonight," I snickered.

Just in time, Attorney Kim passed by.

"Wait in my office," he said to Eliyah.

"Later," she waved at me and scurried away with her cappuccino.

"You have the report I asked you to prepare?" He asked right away.

"Right here, Boss," I said, patting the pile of files on my table.

"Good. The meeting has been rescheduled. Instead of tomorrow, it's to be held at 1 pm. Make sure the necessary files are there," he nodded at me and walked away.

I turned back to my table, going through the files, and checked them once more. I noticed that there were some papers that I needed to make copies of. I headed to the printer and put the papers in. Leaning against the printer, I waited for the copies to be done.

Right then, I heard a ting, signaling a text came in. I unlocked my phone to check. My eyebrows furrowed in confusion. Hmm, weird. This was an unknown number. I clicked on it.

9:10

I have important info about the men you recently arrested. Meet me alone at Boulevard Street in 15 minutes.

I scrutinized the message closely. Who could it be? How did that person know who was arrested? What important information could he have? I replied, asking who they were. I heard a ting instantly.

9:12

Don't waste time. I may be in danger by revealing my identity. This is your last chance. Do not reply again. If you want answers, let's meet up.

I huffed, considering what I should do. I looked at my phone intensely. Then I clicked on Castiel's name. I waited. He didn't pick up. I clicked on

Raphael's name; he was also not picking up. Damn it. They must be in the morning meeting.

I took the copies and rushed to my table. I placed the papers down and ran to Attorney Kim's office. I knocked and entered.

"Boss, I have finished the report preparation. Can I be excused from work for a few minutes?" I asked.

He sat still, staring blankly at me.

"It's urgent!" I added.

"How many minutes?" He finally asked.

"Thirty minutes...maybe," I offered with an awkward chuckle.

Go, be quick!

"Yes, Sir!"

I ran out of the office and down to the parking lot. I saw Eliyah waiting by Mr. Wallace's car. Shit! What do I tell her?

As I passed by her, she looked startled. "What are you doing here?"

"Oh, er...I am going to see Castiel and Raphael! You know they are going to Italy later. I will be busy with work then. Now I'm not, so I'm going, you see, right? Yes, so I better hurry!" I rambled and rushed to my car before she could question me.

I got in my car and waved at Eliyah, who gave me a weird look as I drove by.

I hurried past the streets while I continued glancing at my phone in case of another text. What if it was a prank? But it couldn't be. No one knew who was investigating the case and who got arrested.

I searched for Boulevard street by following the directions since I had never passed through that street before. It was a small street, with only houses around.

Not knowing where to stop, I parked my car on the empty ground near a garage. I stepped out, looking everywhere in suspicion. Whoever it was, I'm sure they would not meet me in public like that.

I continued walking on the sidewalk, looking around.

I tried to call the number that texted me, but I couldn't. Did they block my number?

As I went further, I noticed that there were fewer houses around but more closed-off buildings, which were quiet and seemed empty. Alleys of garbage and abandoned furniture filled in between, giving off a weird smell.

I thought of asking for help, but seeing how people looked at me, I decided against the idea. Some people passing by gave me weird looks like they were wondering what I was doing in this part of the town. I did hear cases of theft were common here, but I only had my phone with me.

Some people passed by me without glancing at me. Some were behind me, and I felt they were scrutinizing me. I tried to look as confident as possible and walked at a slow pace.

Right then, I felt a hand on my shoulder.

That's when I dashed off, letting out a shrill, bloodcurdling scream without looking back.

I ran frantically for some minutes, though I heard no one running after me. In the end, I took a turn and hid in an alley to catch my breath.

I glanced around and saw no one. This seemed like a spooky town. Empty silence, except for some metals clinking here and there, a cat meowing, and a crashing sound of bottles a bit far away.

I should not have come this far. Panicked, I reached out for my phone with a shaking hand and searched for Eliyah's name. I called and waited, taking deep breaths to calm my loud heartbeats.

As I waited, I felt a hand on my shoulder once again. This time, I could not run off. The person pushed me by the shoulder and slammed me against the wall. I felt a sting in my neck. I dropped my phone on the ground, and soon, my body followed. And all light dissolved into darkness.1

☆☆☆

Castiel's perspective

After two hours of discussion and briefing, everyone got out of the meeting room with an exhausted face. I still needed to hurry home to pack since I was to leave in a few hours.

"Hey, wait up!" I heard from behind. I rolled my eyes and continued walking.

A hand flashed in front of me. I pushed the hand aside, scowling at the owner. "What?" I grunted.

"Haelyn called me during the meeting!" Raphael beamed, then he looked confused, "But I called her again and again right now. She isn't picking up." "Why did she need to call again? I thought you already said your goodbyes yesterday," I huffed and walked away.

Raphael ran after me and climbed into the passenger seat of my car. I switched on my phone as I went in and was going to put it back in my pocket when I saw a missed call.

Wait, she called me too?

Raphael glanced at what I was looking for. "Ooh, look! You were grumbling about it, but you were the one she called first," he quipped.

"Shut up," I mumbled and clicked on another message I received.

Eliyah 9:15

Hey, giving you a heads-up. Haelyn will be passing by. ;)

I replied, asking when. I put my phone down and was about to start my car when my phone started ringing. Eliyah's name popped up. Why was she calling instead of texting?

I picked up.

"Haelyn didn't pass by?" was what I heard right away. "Obviously, by my message, you must have understood that she didn't pass by," I replied.

"But she left almost two hours ago, saying that she was going to visit you to say goodbye," I heard her confused voice.

"She didn't come to the office," I mumbled, a bit puzzled. She had no reason to say goodbye, especially to me.

"Attorney Kim called me, saying that she has not returned yet. She called me around an hour ago, but when I called her again, she didn't pick up," Eliyah said, sounding worried now.

"She definitely used me as an excuse to go somewhere else, Eliyah. But if she comes to the office or my apartment, I'll inform you. Bye."

I ran my hand across my hair, annoyed as I cut the call.

That girl always seemed to attract trouble. I hoped she was alright.

I felt myself awaken from the darkness, but my eyes wouldn't open. A heavy feeling in my eyes prevented me from opening them.

I opened up my eyes with great struggle. Everything was blurry. I couldn't differentiate anything from the other. All I saw was a fuzzy haze and a mixture of grey and brown.

Where was I? What happened to me?

Clutching my head tightly, I felt overwhelming fatigue envelop me like a blanket from the coldness that surrounded me.

I moved my hands across the cold floor. The coldness and roughness of its surface washed over my hands. Was I in some sort of basement? How did I end up here?

I pushed my exhausted, trembling hands against the ground so that I could be in a sitting position. It took a great effort to remain sitting, and I waited till my eyesight became clearer. I was able to gradually distinguish my setting. The first thing that caught my eye was the concrete stairs leading up to a closed door. Yup, I was in a basement.

My eyes shot left and right. The basement was pale cream, though a bit dusty around. There were boxes and sacks stacked over each other everywhere. Looking down at my clothes. I realized I was still in my office clothes, but they were soiled and wet. I sniffed at my skirt and quickly put it down. I felt nauseous.

I tried to remember the last thing that had happened to me. I remembered being in another smaller room. It smelled disgusting, and I was constantly moving. Or was it because I felt dizzy and weak?

As I sat pondering what had happened to me, I heard heavy footsteps from above, echoing in the basement. The noise was getting louder, and I heard the jingling of keys.

I flopped back down on the hard, concrete floor, sending another wave of nauseating feelings. I repressed the feeling and closed my eyes, pretending to be unconscious. Pfft, the least they could have done was to give me a bed.

With my ears pressed against the floor, I could hear the footsteps even louder and felt the vibrations of each step. I sensed two men approaching me. I tried my best not to move-

Ouch!

I felt something hit my side, sending a sharp pain throbbing through my body.

D-did that asshole just KICK me?!

I was sure that my eyes were wide open in shock. But they couldn't have seen my reaction since I was facing the other side. I was quite ready to stand up and make them regret messing with me.

"Hmm, she's not waking up. It must have taken a toll on her. I checked on her six hours ago. She hasn't awakened at all."

Instead of standing up as I thought, I stayed still. It? What is it? What did they do to me? And six hours? How long have I been gone for?

"The higher the amount, the longer the effect. Lower the dose now, or just stop giving her. She needs to wake up now," the other man said, but his accent sounded strange. He was definitely a foreigner.

"Why? Will the Boss come to see her? What will Boss do with her?"

"Don't ask too many questions, stupid. Your Boss does not tolerate that," replied the other man mockingly. He didn't seem to like that Boss.

I heard one of them move. I made sure I kept a blank, sleeping face. I felt the knees of whoever moved touching my side. He must have crouched down beside me. I held my breath.

My eyes almost opened when I felt a tug at my hair. The man turned my body around, grabbing my face with his rough hands. I tried not to flinch or twitch in his grasp while biting the insides of my cheek to concentrate on my pretense. He was probably analyzing my condition.

"Tsk, she's so ugly. The drugs must have affected her badly," the man snorted and let go of my face as I hit the floor again.

Oh God, grant me patience! He did not just call me ugly! I did not see him, but he seemed like a shit produced by a deformed cabbage rinsed in vinegar, soaked in cow dung, trampled by a llama, ran over by a tractor, and finally digested by the BigFoot.

But wait! Did he utter the 'd' word? Did he say that I was 'drugged'?

I heard the footsteps now fading away, cut off by the sound of a door slamming shut.

I needed a rest, a long rest to regain my senses. I peacefully closed my eyes again, sending me into a temporary black void.

I felt a tight grip on my hand.

I instantly rolled over, flapping my hands widely. I heard a quiet 'ouch' beside me.

Was it another man attempting to drug me for the hundredth time?

I pushed myself up into a sitting position. With great effort, I opened my eyes, which felt like they were glued together.

"I'll bite you if you take another step," I warned at the blurry image of a tiny form.

As the image became clearer, I looked at the girl beside me.

I scrutinized her, eyeing her from up to down. She looked younger than me and smaller. She wore a blue dress; the blue color was almost invisible with brown and black, dirtying the dress. Her face did not look any better. Red eyes, showing a lack of sleep, stared back at me.

"Phew! I'm not the only one ugly," I croaked, relieved.

"Hey! You don't look any better," the girl retorted, "I mean, look at your clothes. They are torn, muddy, oh, and is that vomit on it? Your hair looks like a bird's nest. Your face looks like a raccoon-"
"Okay, Panda, that's what I meant. You can stop," I said, putting my hand up to halt her praises.

She stopped at once, pursing her lips. I stared at her again. "Who are you?" I finally demanded.

"Leah. You?" she asked in turn.

"Haelyn," I muttered as I crawled on both legs and hands till I reached the wall and leaned back.

"You're British?" she asked with hesitation.

"Duh, what else would I be? And why are you here?"

"Because of my brother."

"You're brother is part of this...group, gang, or whatever it is?"

"Was part of it for a while. He tried leaving, but they wouldn't let him, so he escaped. As a result, I was captured as blackmail. They just transferred me here from another house," she mumbled, looking down at her shaking hands, which she clenched together. "Oh...what will they do with us now?" I asked with apprehension.

Leah shrugged weakly, her eyes getting teary.

"How old are you? You look young," I commented.

"Twenty," she replied. I nodded, and we sat in silence for a few minutes.

I let out a big sigh, attracting her attention back to me.

"Don't just stare. Come here and help me stand up.

We need to get out of here," I said with determination.

Leah quickly stood up, rushing to my side with wide eyes. She grunted and huffed as she dragged me up to my feet. I leaned against the wall; I was too weak right now, but I couldn't wait any longer.

"We can't get out of here, though. The door is locked," Leah muttered, resigned.

"When you were brought here, did you see how the house or building was?" I asked as I rummaged through the boxes.

"Yes, but it's confusing. It resembled a house from the outside, but it is like a complicated labyrinth inside," Leah replied, wearily following my movements.

I hummed as I looked down at the trash in the boxes.

"Did you see any maids around?" I asked again.

"Yeah, some four or five...," Leah drawled and stopped as I removed our new outfits from the box. I threw the clothes at her.

"We need better clothes. Ours are too dirty, and I can't handle the smell anymore," I said, grinning. The clothes were covered with dust, but with some slaps on this side and the other side, the problem was solved.

"Maid clothes, though...?" Leah asked with uncertainty.

"Yup! That's the one we need," I nodded.

We quickly changed and got rid of our clothes, throwing them in the box.

"Now, what?" Leah asked as she fixed the loose outfit, tucking the sides carefully.

I snapped my fingers to the wall on the right side.

"You see that mountain of boxes? We need to move them aside," I said, dragging her by the hand to the boxes.

I tried pushing them, pressing both palms against the boxes. They didn't even move a millimeter. I felt too weak at the moment. There was no strength left in me.

"Let me try," Leah said, pulling up her sleeves as I stepped aside.

I was shaking my head, about to say it was not worth it when I felt a rumble beneath my feet. I looked at that tiny creature in astonishment as she pushed the boxes aside slowly.

"Don't judge by my size," she said smugly. When she finished, she dusted off her hands. Then, she looked at the door next to her, puzzled.

"How did you know there was a door here?" she gasped.

"There seem to be two storerooms linked here. I would sometimes hear loud voices and noises from there, so I took a wild guess," I said, opening the door and walking into the other storeroom.

Leah followed, looking around with wonder. I closed the door behind us. This storeroom was quite different. It was filled with antiquities. Seemed like stolen ones to me.

I spotted the other door. I tried opening it, but it was locked.

"What do we do now?" Leah whispered, walking around, admiring the weird, brown objects.

I took the vase that was on the table beside me. I almost staggered back due to its heavy weight.

I held it steady in my hands and launched at the door. A clattering sound was heard as the door handle broke, falling. The door made a screeching sound as it opened a bit.

"What did you do?" Leah hissed at me. Ignoring her horrified look, I grabbed her hand and dashed out.

I ran through the corridors, doing zigzags, hitting walls here and there. The dizziness was catching up on me. But I did not care about finding the right way as long as we got away from what I just did. I was sure the noise attracted someone's attention.

As I made another turn, I froze in place in front of the mammoth.

"Che cosa era quel suono?" the man grunted, his black eyes eyeing both Leah and me, with intensity.

Wait, what? Another foreigner?

"Una scatola cadde."

I glanced at Leah in surprise, my eyes asking her, 'You speak Italian too?'.

The man grumbled something and walked away.

"Hey, you can sp-"

Before I could continue, Leah pushed me against a wall, her finger over her mouth, asking me to keep quiet. I nodded and waited as I heard some voices approaching. We waited till the voices faded away.

"One of the men that passed by was the one who brought me here. We need to hurry. I feel like they'll find out about our escape real soon," Leah whispered, throwing an anxious look around.

"Let's walk in the direction from where they came from, the main door must be there," I said as we crept against the wall, silently but hastily.

We arrived in a spacious room, where Leah halted my steps. "This is where I entered earlier," she mumbled.

"Let's get out then," I said. Glancing left and right for any sign of people, we ran to the door. Thankfully, that one was not locked.

I staggered in my footsteps after I closed the door. I raised my hands in the air, whispering freedom to myself.

A shout from inside cut my happiness. I exchanged worried looks with Leah.

I looked here and spotted a large plant pot. "Hey, superwoman! Help me push this to block the door. It can help distract them for a few seconds at least," I said.

With Leah's help, I managed to drag the pot and push it against the door.

"Let's go!" I said, running down the stairs.

"Stanno scappando!" I heard a shout from inside.

They must have seen us from the windows.

I heard a gunshot. It weirdly gave me a flashback of a similar incident some weeks ago.

Then I heard another gunshot. And another.

Leah grasped my hands, encouraging me to run faster. But another fatigue was catching up on me. I was so high I couldn't even understand anything that was happening. It felt like everything was fading in the background.

I felt something graze my arm as it left a burning sensation. I gathered all the strength left in me as I ran faster.

"Let's get in the car across the street and drive away!" I yelled, between heavy breaths, pointing to the black car.

"What if it's locked?" Leah yelled back.

"We stop a car, drag the driver out, and escape!"

As I crossed the street, I slammed my hand against the door, scrambling around, reaching for the car handle. I pulled, and the car door opened.

"Hey! It's unlocked! Jump in," I exclaimed in excitement.

I sat in, with a confused Leah jumping in the seat beside me. We needed to get away. No time to wear seatbelts.

I reached out for the steering wheel and the gear lever but got nothing. I looked down to see that there was no steering wheel. Was I so high that I was being delusional?

Before I could say anything, I heard a gun cocked and froze.

"Hands up!" I heard from behind.

I gulped and held my breath. Despite all my efforts, we got caught!

I hesitatingly looked around, and a loud gasp escaped my mouth as my eyes widened. And so was the reaction of the man behind.

"Raphael?!"

I couldn't believe my eyes. I was abducted and drugged. I tried to escape and saw Raphael pointing a gun at me. Or was this all a dream?

"Haelyn? Is that you? What happened to you? You stink!" Raphael exclaimed with a grimace.

I frowned and pushed his gun away from me.

"What are you doing here? Aren't you supposed to be gone to Italy?" I asked, scowling.

Raphael stared at me with a weird expression. Leah also stared at me.

"Uhmm, Haelyn...we are in Italy right now," Leah said.

I gaped back at them. I shook my head repeatedly, trying to refresh my memory.

"No, no, this can't be another hallucination. I remember clearly that I was in London when I was abducted," I blurted.

"We definitely are in Italy right now though. And do you know that man? Is he dangerous?" Leah whispered, leaning towards me.

"Well, he's got a gun. You can judge for yourself," I said, groaning as I leaned against the door.

Then a gunshot made me jump back straight.

"I forgot we needed to escape!" I screeched and turned to Raphael, "What are you waiting for? I don't know why you're here, but I've got my life to save. Either you get down here, and I drive away, or you drive."

I glanced outside and was surprised to see no one coming out. But I could still hear the firing of guns. What was happening?

"We planned to infiltrate the place secretly, but they must have been alerted early due to your escape. They cannot come out, though. Some men of ours have been placed around," Raphael assured us.

"Oh, you came to save me?" I beamed.

"No, we didn't know you were here or have been abducted, as you're saying," Raphael said, throwing me a confused look.

I sighed. So that's how it was.

"Actually, Eliyah received a message from you a week earlier, you said that you were going to come to Italy," he added.

"A week! You mean to say a week has passed-"

Right at the moment of my confusion and disbelief, the door next to Raphael opened.

"They are escaping from the back. We need to."

I peeped out of my seat, waving at Castiel with a grin. "Wait, wh-? You?" he spluttered and looked at Raphael for an explanation for that miracle.

"She was held hostage here...," he replied, shrugging.

He closed the door and opened the one next to me. The one I was leaning against. I instantly leaned out, about to fall out.

Castiel pushed me back inside and scrutinized me.

"For how many days did you not shower?" he frowned.

Wow, I was getting a lot of compliments today. I didn't even bother replying.

"And are you bleeding?" he said and was about to touch me when I slapped his hand away.

"I think a bullet may have grazed my arm, not that it concerns you. You should just stay away since I stink," I rolled my eyes.

"And who is that?" Castiel asked me, finally noticing Leah, who looked intimidated by Castiel's gaze or glare on her.

"She was abducted by those goons as well," I shrugged.

Castiel closed the door again and moved to the other side. He opened Leah's door.

"Move at the back. I'm driving," he ordered.

Leah quickly nodded and scurried to the back beside Raphael.

"What about the others?" Raphael asked.

"They can handle it," Castiel muttered and glanced at me, "Do not sleep. We'll arrive at the hospital soon."

I chuckled. He knew I liked doing everything that people told me not to.

So yeah, I closed my eyes and slept.

☆☆☆

I finally opened my eyes again. A white ceiling greeted me. I moved around on the other side. The bed was quite soft. I close my eyes in relaxation.

I frowned as I felt a pain searing in my right arm. I sat up in bed and touched my arm; it was bandaged. Then, I remembered what had happened.

I got out of bed and noticed no shoes or slippers. I looked around; the room had another bed beside mine, and there were two tables beside each bed.

I moved to the door and was going to get out, but then I paused. I probably looked like a maniac right now, and I stank. I had to shower first. Or maybe brush my teeth first. When was the last time I went to the toilet?

I went to the bathroom and looked down; I had no clothes other than the hospital gown I was wearing. I guessed I would have to wear it again. I quickly took a shower, went to the toilet, and brushed my teeth with a toothbrush that I hoped was new.

I brushed my hand through my wet hair. Thank God, it stopped smelling like a sewer.

I opened the door and saw Castiel leaning against the wall. I quickly took a step away from him.

"It's okay. You no longer stink," he chuckled.

I glared at him and threw the wet towel on him. He caught it easily and threw it in the laundry basket inside the bathroom.

"The doctor said that you should not walk around.

You need rest, so get in bed, Princess," he mockingly gestured for me to follow him to the bed.

"It's Queen to you, peasant," I rolled my eyes and flipped my wet hair at him.

I lay down on the bed, covering myself with the light blanket and getting comfortable. I closed my eyes; I was quite ready for yet another sleep.

I heard a strong rumble. I opened up my eyes.

"Was that an earthquake?" I whispered.

"No, that was your stomach," Castiel said as he sat on the opposite bed, staring at me.

"Oh, my hearing sense must have heightened up," I claimed, sitting up.

"Not really. I'm sure the patient next door heard it too," Castiel mused.

I glared at him. My shoulders slumped. I need pizza. I need strength.

I glanced at Castiel, and my eyes went to the table next to him. There was something in that paper bag. I eyed his amused look and the bag.

"What's that?" I mumbled, trying to reach for it, but I got my hands slapped away.

"Pizza. BBQ chicken pizza."

My hands desperately reached for it and missed again as Castiel took it away.

"Don't you have anything to say to me before?" he raised an eyebrow at me.

I glanced at the pizza. I was salivating.

"Uhm...I love you?" I made an attempt.

Castiel's expression changed from smug to constipated and then to a glare. I didn't wait for his reply and grabbed the pizza from his grasp.

I took a heavenly bite before Castiel could take it away from me. He continued glaring at me. His glare was disturbing my appetite.

"What? You want?" I asked, with my mouth full.

"You joke about love a lot, huh?" he muttered.

I stopped eating and looked at him. "When did I joke about that to you before?" I asked.

"Remember? The prank you pulled the second year of high school?" he scoffed.

"What prank?" I asked, confused.

"You wrote a love letter or poem and signed it with your name at the bottom. Then, you put it in my book. When I asked you about it, you brushed me off, saying you never did such a thing," he rolled his eyes.

"That's because I really did not," I said, scowling.

"I know your writing, Haelyn, and it was the paper with a flower imprinted on it that you usually used back then," he said firmly.

"Oh...was it the light cream paper?"

"Yes."

"In a red envelope?"

"Yes."

"Was it a poem that covered half the page?"

"Yes."

"That was not for you," I concluded.

"Uh?"

"That was for Embry," I laughed, taking another bite from the pizza.

"You...love my brother?" he asked, cringing.

I coughed on the pizza, shaking my head vigorously. Embry was Castiel's brother, only a year younger than us. Surprisingly, I went along with him better than with Castiel. And there was no way that I loved him.

"Are you kidding me? He's younger than me!" I exclaimed. "He said that he needed a fake love letter for a prank, so I-"

I stopped midway, exchanging looks with Castiel as I realized. Oh...a prank. To whom? I just found out now.

I let out an awkward laugh as Castiel let out a curse under his breath that I couldn't decipher.

"It's not like you believe it, though, right?" I shrugged.

"What?"

"I love you."

An audible gasp echoed. My eyes roamed to the now-opened door, where a group of agents and Leah followed inside.

"See, I told you guys! They love each other!" Raphael exclaimed, doing a celebratory dance around the room. Everyone facepalmed at his foolishness.

"Congratz, babez!" He said to me and took a slice of pizza, sitting on my bed with one arm around my shoulder.

Leah stood awkwardly in the middle of the big agents standing in front of my bed. She was now dressed in clean, casual clothes. I ushered her to the other side of my bed.

"Are you okay?" she whispered.

"No, the hospital gown sucks," I whispered back.

"I bought clothes for you to change into. That man paid," she said, handing me a bag and pointing to Shooky. "Thanks, Shooky!" I winked at him as he rolled his eyes toward me.

"By the way, are you still high?" Raphael asked. I glowered at him.

"Calm down. I'm just asking because the doctor said that there was GHB left in your system."

"Do you remember anything from the past few days?" one of the agents asked. I sighed. Was I a witness yet again?

"No, I just remember being in a different basement or room. And there was a constant dizzy feeling," I said, shaking my head.

The men exchanged looks in silence. Can't they discuss it orally for once?

"We believe those who abducted you were involved in drug trafficking and thefts of valuable objects. You were probably brought here along with the last shipment of drugs," Cooky concluded.

I imagined the thought of me being parcelled along with containers of stolen things and drugs on a ship and instantly shuddered. That must have been the dizzy moving motions that I remembered faintly. "Okay, cool. No one was suspicious about my disappearance?" I asked.

"Eliyah had called me asking if you came to the office," I ignored Castiel's look as I waited for him to continue, "She called again in the evening, saying that she got a text from you, which said that you also left for Italy. Then she could not get in contact with your phone again," he finished.

Oh no, my phone! It must have been thrown away somewhere. All the important things that were stored in it are gone. But the most important one is my memes! Just poof!

"What do I do now?" I huffed.

"You'll stay here for a few days to rest. Right now, you have no phone, no money, no passport or papers to be able to go back. We'll try to prepare papers for you to return home, but it'll take time," Castiel replied.

"How about her?" I asked, pointing to Leah.

"I've contacted her brother. I think it's best for both of them to move away, somewhere more secure back in England," Raphael replied and turned to Leah, "I heard that your maternal grandmother lives in Manchester. You should stay there for a while." Leah nodded quietly.

I cleared my throat and got ready to ask the question. "And...where will I stay?"

"Castiel has two rooms at his place. I'm sure he can lend you one," Raphael·said, trying to look nonchalant, but I could see his smirk.2 "Yeah, okay. So it's decided!" Shooky said, clapping his hands for our attention before we could start another debate. "We need to get going now. We still have work to do. If you could follow me," he gestured to Leah as the others stepped out of the room.

Leah turned to me and gave me a farewell hug.

"Don't worry, and stay safe. I'll contact you once I return home," I patted her back comfortingly. She returned my smile and followed Shooky out.

"So, can I go already? Help me out!" I demanded, asking for Raphael's help, as I took the bag of clothes in one hand.

I turned to Castiel as we were leaving. "Don't forget the pizza!"

☆☆☆

I walked around the streets of Naples, taking pictures from my new brand phone that Castiel bought. He made sure I understood that it was not a gift and that I had to return the money.

The camera was awesome; it was my first time outside Castiel's apartment since my arrival. I spent the past three days in my temporary room, forced to rest. I also had to explain the situation to Eliyah and my Dad, who was almost packing for Italy when I told them what happened.

Then, I had to call Attorney Kim, who kept on complaining about how I was stupid to walk willingly into the enemy's net and how he had to handle so much work alone.

Back in Naples, I came to a standstill at the poster that attracted my attention. It was an art exhibition poster. I couldn't understand anything. I scanned the poster, looking for the venue. San Carlo seemed to be the road where it was held.

I used Google maps to search for the road as I walked around.

After some five minutes, I reached the sign of an art gallery. It seemed like a public gallery, considering how people kept flowing in and out. I also followed them in.

Paintings covering the white walls surrounded the spacious room. I did not know much about art, but I liked them as long as they attracted my attention. I didn't forget to take pictures of the ones I liked best.

I walked to the end of the hall. The last painting captured my attention. It was a painting of multiple hands covered in filth and soot from the darkness, reaching out to touch a little girl holding a lantern, which illuminated where she was standing.

I stepped back to get the whole painting in my picture when I knocked against someone from behind. I immediately turned around, apologizing. It was a young woman wearing a formal, black halter dress that complimented her long black hair and green eyes. The woman chuckled and shook her head.

"Va bene. It's okay. I saw you admiring my painting," she smiled, gesturing to the piece of art. I nodded at her.

"It's great. You have awesome talent!" I complimented.

"Thank you. I'm Angelia," she said, stretching out her hand.

"Haelyn," I replied, shaking her hand.

I heard someone calling her name from behind. She nodded at them and looked back at me. "It was nice meeting you. This exhibition is being held for a few days. I hope you can come again," she smiled and walked away.

I took a picture of the painting and looked at the time. I should be returning now. I walked back to Castiel's apartment leisurely, admiring everywhere. It was rare to get a holiday, so I might as well make the most out of it.

I arrived right in time to see Castiel get into the car he had been renting. I jogged to his side.

"Where are you going? Can I come along?" I asked immediately.

He frowned at me. "Where's Claudius?" he questioned. I pointed to the agent following me the whole day, standing still far away.

"He's shy, so he made sure he remained at least five meters behind me," I commented.

Okay, good. Go up," Castiel said.

"No, I'm coming along!" Before he could lock the door, I slipped into the passenger seat.

"Don't you ever get enough of the trouble you always get into?" Castiel asked with an annoyed sigh. "You mean there is trouble where you're going?" I asked excitedly.

"Why are you like this?" Castiel seemed to be questioning my weird existence.

"I was born like this. Let's just go. I promise I'll stick by your side."

Castiel finally started the car. He must have thought it was too much of a heavy task to drag me back to his place.

I attached my seatbelt, grinning as we moved forward.

I didn't forget to wave at Claudius, who looked like he was relieved of a burden of duty.

"That's illegal."

"Yes, I know."

"What are we doing here, then?"

I did not get a reply. I looked around from far outside the crowd. I could hear a mix of cheers and groans. Some people were still waiting outside in groups. Others were sitting in the middle of the road, smoking. It looked like weed because two had their faces planted on the road. Even the air around stank.

I heard roars of excitement, and I peered inside to see what was going on. It seemed like someone had finally won. "Aren't you a law enforcement agent? You should not be participating in such activities," I said, turning around and realizing that I was talking to the air. Where did Castiel disappear, leaving me alone in such a place? Did he abandon me to die here?

I walked back and forth, peeking here and there, hoping to see him, but he seemed to have disappeared into thin air.

I couldn't even ask around because of the stares I was receiving. They must have been wondering what I was doing there.

Thankfully, the car was still there. I stood by the car, waiting. There was a man nearby, sitting on the ground near the pavement. I glanced at him as I caught him staring at me. I looked again, and he was still staring. Did he want to say something?

"Beautiful night today, right?" I chuckled at him, "It's a great night for a...joint, yes." I eyed him with pursed lips as he smoked a joint and paused again, staring at me again. Okay...weird.

I leaned against the car door and checked if it was unlocked. Just by awesome chance, it was locked.

I looked around, hoping there was another escape in case of an unfortunate incident. I glanced at the man again and saw him flopped unconscious on the pavement. Oh, how relatable. Brought back memories of a few days ago.

I gasped in relief as I saw Shooky approaching me. I ran to him, clutching his arm.

"I appoint you as my bodyguard for tonight," I started and paused, "Do you do those things as well?"

"What? And can you ease up on the arm? You're pinching me," he requested with a grimace.

"Did you come to bet?" I said as I loosened my hold on him.

"No," he frowned at me.

"Then, what are we doing here?" I asked.

"Let's go in," he said, marching into the fight club. With my hand clutching him, I got dragged along.

The place was hot and stuffy. The men snarled at me as I got knocked against them while trying to follow Shooky. Italian remarks flew around wildly; I was sure they were curses. My small self squeezed through the men until I arrived at the first few rows.

A man came on stage; it must have been the announcer. The next contestants were being announced. I didn't pay attention since I did not understand.

"Why are we watching this? Is this how you agents learn how to fight?" I whispered to Shooky. He glanced at me and looked up at the fight ring again. I huffed and looked back onstage, and my mouth went agape.

I rubbed my eyes and looked up again.

Castiel, you idiot! What are you doing up there? I wanted to yell at him. But he didn't even spare me a glance.

I looked to the opposite side of the ring and gulped at his opponent's sight. He was about the same height as Castiel, but he was...large. His muscles seemed to be bouncing as he moved. And tattoos made their way around his bald head, down his shoulders and arms. He must have been a popular one around, seeing that everyone was cheering for him, not that the cheers affected Castiel in any way. Instead, he remained his usual composed self.

Just as the whistle blew, Castiel went down like a leaf.

I screeched loudly, not that anyone heard me among the other men's loud cheering. The man tackled Castiel down mercilessly, throwing punches repeatedly. Castiel took the first punch but, by reflex, was able to block the rest. With one swift kick from Castiel, the Godzilla staggered back a few steps. But it did not last long. The man dashed forward, using his whole weight to throw Castiel to the other side of the ring. I sighed at this. Why was Castiel doing nothing except trying to look weak and being only in defensive mode? Each time his opponent attacked, he took a step back, waited for another attack, and dodged again.

Everyone was booing at him. My glares went undetected.

But Castiel remained blank as he eyed Godzilla up and down in a calculating way. I could see the enemy getting more frustrated as time went by. And his attacks became less precise, and he acted more briskly.

As Godzilla was about to swing one more punch, Castiel went under, delivering a short sidekick, and rushed behind his rival, who went down on one knee. Without sparing a second, Castiel shoved him to the ground.

The fallen man stood up with a groan. He was fuming as he roared out some beautiful Italian words I couldn't understand. He tried jumping on Castiel and launching a kick but missed. Castiel went back to his dodging game.

I sighed. It no longer felt scary to me. It seemed as if Castiel was testing his rival's patience and messing with him.

"Finish it already!" I yelled. The other men yelled out as well. We shared the same opinions, except we were rooting for different men.

Castiel smirked and raised his fists, ready for attack. Castiel repeated his earlier move, delivering a hard kick, aiming for the other knee as the opponent turned around to send a kick. This propelled Godzilla back to the ground.

As he was standing up, I noticed his legs trembling. Then, I understood what Castiel was trying to do. He must have observed how his rival used his weight on his legs as the base and stance for all his attacks. If his legs were weakened, his tactics would follow.

Before the man could stand up, Castiel launched a kick to his stomach, propelling him to the ground. There were a lot of 'ooh's going around as I winced at the sight of the poor man, who didn't seem to have given up.

His eyes were like blazing fire while Castiel gave him an ice-cold look. With fury, he advanced toward Castiel. This time, finally, Castiel went into attack mode, serving a full course of quality punches, one after another.

Now, everyone went silent; they seemed worried. It was easy to guess who they bet on. I sighed.

I should have put some money into that match as well. "Let's go out," Shooky said, in a bored tone, turning around. I zigzagged my way out through the mass quietly. And as I reached outside, I heard a chorus of groans erupt, which caused a grin to spread on my face. I didn't need to turn around and see who won.

I waited outside beside the car. Castiel joined us after a few minutes.

"Aaay, man! Highfi-" I looked at his bloody hands and retracted mine to my side as Castiel came closer.

"It was awesome!" I exclaimed, patting his back, and again, I quickly withdrew my hand as I noticed him wincing.

I looked between the two men and waited. One thing I learned over the past few weeks is not to expect an answer to my question, so asking questions is useless.

A dark-haired, young guy approached us. The first thing I noticed about him was a load of cash in his hand. I must have had the dollar sign expression in my eyes as I fixed my gaze on him.

"Grazie. Seguimi," he nodded at Castiel and walked away.

"Wait for me. I'll talk to him and come back," Shooky said and followed the young boy.

"Get in," Castiel said, walking to the other side and entering. I also opened the door and followed.

"So...I didn't know you were into this. Your job doesn't pay enough?"

Castiel seemed to want to argue against me but cut to the chase, "That boy is an informant. He wanted to trade information with this." "And he got all that money from this one fight?" I asked. Castiel nodded. Damn, he could have split.

I noticed Castiel's bloody, literally bloody hands as I looked down. He didn't even clean up. I slipped my hands into my back pocket, reaching for my handkerchief.

I grasped his arm, getting a startled look from him. I grabbed the water bottle and let the liquid flow on the handkerchief. I swiped both hands around, making sure there was nothing left. I turned his hands to check if they were clean. Oh my God, I'm so weird, but his hands are quite pretty. I placed his hands back on him after admirin- cleaning them.

Castiel stared at me quizzically.

"You have to drive. You can't get the car bloody, you know," I said.

He hummed in agreement, but I saw his hidden expression.

"Don't act like this. Stop smiling at me," I scoffed and looked away.

☆☆☆

"Who is Alessio Verdino?" I asked.

Everyone was deep in thought as they ignored my question.

I looked at Raphael, who was also looking around. Answer me!

I don't know either, was the reply sent by telepathy?

I looked at the time; it was 11 pm. The team was having a brief meeting in Castiel's living room. Shooky translated everything that boy told him. Apparently, Argus was his friend and had informed him that he had made a deal with someone called Alessio. And almost everyone seemed to be aware of who he was. "He must have joined another gang. It makes no sense for the Verdinos to be still around," one of the team members said.

I opened my mouth to ask a question again but closed it. Instead, I switched on my phone and went to google. I typed 'Verdino' and got some random shit. I should search for something more specific. I added crime and gang to the search bar.

Oh, there were some articles! But they were from years back.

I browsed through the titles of the articles. Hmm, okay, the titles revealed enough. They were not a gang but a mafia organization! Ooh, the Italian mafia, they were always famous, or should I say, infamous.

I cleared my throat and looked at everyone. "What happened to the Verdinos after the Boss died?"

How-

I pointed to my phone, which Raphael grabbed from me and started reading.

"Usually, when the Boss dies, one of the family members takes his position. But after Enzo Verdino, the Boss died, all their activities stopped. We rarely ever heard of them after that. Most members of the mafia left as well," Shooky explained. "Oh, I remember!" Raphael said, snapping his fingers. "I heard about it from someone. They said that, after the Boss died, many illegal activities that took place on a local and global scale decreased drastically."

"Definitely because the Verdinos were among the main organizations involved in multiple illegal trades with other main organizations. Like the international drug trade, imports and exports decreased by 20% due to them going 'extinct,'" Castiel explained. "But did they? Or was it only a facade, and they are planning something?" I whispered, adding my comment to build the necessary suspense.

Castiel rolled his eyes at me.

"I think the reason they went down silently like that has to do with the death of Enzo Verdino. His death remains a mystery to this day. How did he die? I'm sure there would have been some revenge if it was a rival mafia or gang. Or if it was a natural death, there could have been an internal war for who will take his place," Raphael commented.

"If we get hold of Alessio, maybe we'll know. After all, he was supposed to claim Enzo's position after he died. This makes me wonder why he approached Argus for this deal. He's up to something," Cooky muttered.

"We should inform Mr. Ford and see about it tomorrow. And we have to run the profiles of some past members of the Verdino mafia through the Italian police and tell them to notify us if any activities by these people are detected," Cooky said, standing up. The others followed along.

☆☆☆

Why does Castiel have a fridge when he keeps nothing in it? I huffed as I took the elevator down.

I halted by the vending machine. I felt the money in my purse bursting with excitement. Ooh yeah, another expenditure! I knelt, eyeing my choices. I selected a pack of gummies and a coke. I inserted the money and waited.

I frowned as nothing came out. I clicked again, and nothing came out. I tapped it lightly and still had the same disappointing result. My money was long gone.

"Do you need some help?" I heard from above.

I looked up to see a man looking down at me. He had a bit of stubble, with an undercut hairstyle, his brown hair thrown towards the back. The sun seemed to lighten his already bright grey eyes.

"Woah, you're handsome," I breathed out.

"That's not the answer to my question," he raised an eyebrow at me.

I flushed red. I stood up and nodded, motioning to the vending machine. I wondered what magic he was going to perform. He glanced at the vending machine from both sides. He turned around, and with one swift kick to the side, both products I bought popped out.

I grabbed both quickly before the devilish vending machine could try to swallow them back. I glanced up to see the man already leaving.

"Hey!" I yelled as he turned back around.

"Thanks! How did you know I was not Italian?" I asked.

"I saw you with those British agents and took a guess.

I also live in this building," he shrugged.

"Cool, I hope to see you again," I smiled.

"Maybe. You seem to be a first-time visitor here. It's quite dangerous around here. I hope you are careful and do not trust anyone easily," he stated seriously and marched away.

"Okay," I mumbled to myself as he left. It seemed like he wanted to say something more. And, oh! I didn't even get to know his name. Bummer.

I walked down the road as I glanced at my phone. I felt lazy today; I didn't want to walk. I should call a taxi and then walk back after.

I hailed one after waiting for some five minutes.

"Dove vuoi andare?" the taxi driver asked as I got in.

I showed him the poster of the art exhibition, and he nodded.

I arrived quite fast, in ten minutes. I got down and glanced around. The place was crowded as usual. I peeped inside and saw that there were fewer people inside rather than outside.

A tap on the shoulder made me jump around to face Angelina, the painter I met the other day.

"You came again," she smiled brightly.

"Were you going in as well?" I asked.

"No, actually, since it's lunchtime, most people left. So I was heading out for lunch as well. Would you join me if you want to grab lunch first?" she asked.

I pondered over it. I was quite hungry as well, seeing that I skipped breakfast. Not that it was a rare occurrence anyway.

"Gladly," I answered.

We walked down the street to a small restaurant, Pasta la Vista. We sat at the tables available outside, beside the busy streets.

"La Campania is crowded all day, but it's a bit more during lunch. Believe me, though, it's less stuffy outside," Angelia said, chuckling as we looked at the flow of people around.

I looked at the menu; lasagne, spaghetti, tetrazzini, pasta primavera, and more made me salivate. I closed my eyes and flipped to a random page to choose. Okay, carbonara, it was.3 "So, are you from around here itself, or did you come here only for the art exhibit? " I asked as we waited.

"Oh, I'm from Napoli itself, and I am also one of the main organizers of this exhibit," Angelia replied.

"So painting is your full-time job?"

"Hmm, yes. That's somewhat the case," she nodded.

Her paintings were very good, and she seemed to be well-known around. I glanced at her clothes. Was that Gucci?

"And it pays well," she winked at me, and I grinned in response.

"And what about you?" she asked, leaning forward, clasping her hands together.

"Nothing great. Just a paralegal at a law firm," I shrugged.

"That's still good, as long as you have the ambition to rise the levels," she nodded.

"Definitely," I smiled in agreement. Just in time, our meals arrived.

We continued our conversation throughout the meal as I inquired about her journey as an artist. I also learned she was 28 years old, a bit older than me, and did Fine Arts at university. She talked a lot about Naples, advising me where to visit.

We stood up to head to the exhibit when we finished eating and paying. But a text interrupted me.

Castiel 12:30

Return. Now.

I texted him right away, asking why, but being the annoying self that he was, he didn't text back. I rolled my eyes at my phone and sighed as Angelia raised a questioning eyebrow at me.

"I'm sorry, a...friend texted me saying that there is some urgent matter to take care of, so I need to return," I gave an apologetic smile.

She shook her head. "No worries. Maybe we could meet up another time while you're still in Italy. Can we exchange phone numbers?"

"Sure," I said, handing my phone as she inserted her number.

I took a taxi back to the apartment. I wondered why Castiel wanted me back. He usually preferred that the 'pest' stay out all day.

I got out of the car and headed back to the building. "Hey!" someone shouted from behind.

I turned around and saw the man from the morning. He approached me and handed me what I believed was my earphones.

"I was parking here and saw those falling on the ground," he explained.

"Thanks," I answered and glanced at his parked black van.

"What's your name, by the way?" I asked.

"Why?" He frowned questioningly.

"Why not?" I asked, frowning in return.

"What if I don't wanna reveal my identity?" He shrugged.

"Then you're suspicious. Are you a spy? Or are you one of those strangers roaming around in a black van, kidnapping people?" I raised an eyebrow.

"You seem to overthink a lot. Even if I was one of these, would I say that I am?" He shrugged, a tiny mocking smile on his face.

"Well, you got the point, so-"

"Who are you talking to?" Castiel's voice resounded as he came to stand by my side.

I gulped and turned to him with a smile. "A neighbor of yours," I replied as his eyes narrowed at the man.

The man was not intimidated by Castiel. Instead, he shrugged, muttered something in Italian, and walked away. I didn't get his name yet again.

"Why did you tell me to return?"

"Get in my car," Castiel said, walking past me. I jogged after catching up.

"Why? Are we going on a date?" I joked.

My face hit Castiel's back as he stopped in front of the car.

"Why? You want to?" came the dry response.

"With you? Anytime," I laughed, getting in the car as I got an eye roll in return from him.

☆☆☆

"I thought you said the IOF has no headquarters here," I commented as we entered the elevator.

"This is just an office for meetings within ourselves or with other people. Most countries have at least this," Castiel replied.

"What am I doing here, then? Ain't this supposed to be a meeting between you all?"

"Because I can't trust you with your own life," Castiel said as we got out of the elevator. I scoffed behind him; I couldn't even refute him.

A long table and a large screen were positioned in front of it. I got pushed to a seat by Castiel, at the corner of the room, outside the group. I frowned at him.

"You're making me an outcast."

"That's what you are. Just remain quiet and wait till we finish," he smirked, and to irk me more, he had to pat my head, not once, but TWICE. That was the limit.

I positioned my leg high and kicked as he turned to the table. I was honestly aiming for his leg, but sometimes, I get better results than the effort I put in.

So I kicked his ass, literally.

I was unsure if it hurt, but he paused for a second. As he stood rigidly, it seemed that some steam was coming out from both of his ears. Yup, he was furious.

Just then, Mr. Ford entered, followed by other agents. He motioned to Castiel to sit down. Without looking at me, he marched towards the table and sat down. Meanwhile, I pressed my lips firmly as I cackled mentally. I felt like I was going to regret it later.

I dragged my chair to the window, looking out, so I did not feel awkward.

Fifteen minutes later, I gradually moved close enough to stick myself between them.

"We have plotted around ten men in different harbors to watch out for any more suspicious ships. Even some of your team members were appointed around the Naples' harbors," Mr. Ford explained.

I looked around and counted. I noticed that four men were missing, including Raphael.

"And did you get any information about Alessio Verdino?" Mr. Ford asked.

"There were no sightings of him for some weeks. And we inquired about past members of the mafia from the local police. They said that most of them have disappeared completely while others have joined small gangs around. If the Verdinos are rising, they may be controlling their activities secretly," Cooky said.

"What if it's not just everyone but Alessio planning something?" another agent asked.

We all paused and contemplated the idea.

"Even if he's the leader or something, he can't be doing anything alone. The fact that he can control the activities even if they occur in other countries is something to consider. He or his group has contacts everywhere," Mr. Ford replied.

I raised my hand. Mr. Ford raised an eyebrow at me.

"I'm just curious. How many family members of the Verdinos were in the mafia?"

"We don't know, actually. We know Alessio because he was already exposed to this world back then and was expected to be the one taking over after his father," Mr. Ford said.

"There have been rumors that he does have other siblings, though. And Enzo's wife had died long ago. And since Enzo was an orphan, there are no wider kins of his," Castiel added.

"What we need to do right now is to search who is with Alessio and what is their real aim. Make sure to pass the message to all police stations to keep a lookout for any suspicious activities," Mr. Ford stated.

After a few more minutes of briefing and suggesting what to do and where to go, it was time to leave. I ran ahead first and got into Castiel's car first.

Castiel got in and gave me a dead stare. I looked to my right side, ignoring him. His hand slamming against my window startled me, and as I turned, I was met with his face, only an inch away from me. I gulped as the sense of being caged enveloped me.

"Can you, like, get away?" I croaked, pushing him out of my comfort zone.

He smirked, his hand reaching out to grab mine, which was pressing on his shoulder. He squeezed my hand and whispered in my ear, "I'll get you back when the right time comes." And as he withdrew his face away, his cold lips brushed against my cheek, leaving shivers in me. Shivers that I got from cringing so hard.

He retracted to his seat, and I got my confidence back. "Ha, you can try," I scoffed.

A smirking Castiel ignored me and started the car.

As Castiel was parking his car, I unfastened my seatbelt.

"Oh, there goes your neighbor again!" I exclaimed, seeing the stranger. He was walking to his black van, sporting black jeans and a jacket, followed by another man, whom I couldn't see from my perspective.

His van was parked at the end of the line, and as he passed by, Castiel pushed my head, making me duck down as the men passed by, making both of our heads crash together.

"What are you doing?" I hissed.

"Wait a few seconds," Castiel whispered. I huffed and stayed still.

When he rose up again, I followed and glared at him, searching for an explanation. But he wasn't looking at me. Instead, his eyes were focused on the strangers. I squinted my eyes towards them as they arrived at the van, standing and discussing something.

"Hey! Isn't that the Italian guy? His name was Bocal something!" I exclaimed, gaping at him.

"Boccaccio, Giuseppe Boccaccio," Castiel muttered.

"Yeah, that's it. You guys sent him back. And I know you didn't send him back only because he was an undocumented migrant. What was the real reason?" I narrowed my eyes at him.

"We've been keeping tabs on him ever since he arrived. While he probably thought that we helped him walk free, he's been helping us indirectly," Castiel shrugged. I hummed in agreement. Good tactic.

"But if he's really guilty of being linked to the cases and is with this guy, does that mean this man too...?" I trailed in realization. "Damn, but he's handsome, though," I huffed in disappointment.

"What are you implying?" came the ice-cold question. "Nothing. Let's follow them," I brushed him off and gestured to the men, getting in the van. If our assumptions were right, it must have really been a van used to kidnap people.

Castiel sighed and started the car again, ready for another ride.

"Should we inform the others?" I asked.

"No, we do not know where they are heading or what they are doing for certain yet," Castiel replied, concentrating on the van in front of us.

I was going to comment that they'll spot us but stopped as Castiel took a left turn while the van went right ahead. He knew his shit, so I'll leave him to it. I shrugged to myself.

We drove for a long hour and finally slowed down as we approached the sound of waves. While the van continued, Castiel parked the car in an alley. We got down, and the salty breeze was the first thing that hit me.

"Let's go," Castiel declared, jogging ahead as I ran after him, clutching my purse and squeezing it in my pocket.

Soon, we approached the harbor; the sound of the waves resounded in my ears while some seagulls screeched, swooping up in the air. And at that moment, I wished I could take a picture of the setting sun at sea. A mix of purple and orange seemed to have been thrown across the sky, which reflected on the sea, where a few yachts were floating on the horizon.

Castiel's hand dragged me back to reality. His hand was grasping mine tightly as I looked up at him. He was not looking at me.

"Stay close. I don't want you running about and risking getting shipped away again," he said seriously.

I opened my mouth to reply.

"And do not speak. You'll attract unwanted attention." I closed my mouth.

The harbor was quite animated at this time of the day, perhaps due to our beautiful view. Castiel and I walked, hand in hand, besides the harbor, where the boats bobbed and creaked, along with the motion of the slight waves.

The boats and ships seemed to be lined up by size. Small boats and yachts filled the view around us, but further ahead lay the cargo ships, fishing vessels, and bulk carriers.

Soon, the sun disappeared beyond the ocean, dragging the colorful sky away. A dull grey color replaced the earlier breathtaking view while the chilly breezes of the night set in. Most people were turning around to leave while we moved along the harbor, going deeper into where the bigger ships lay about.

Castiel paused in his steps behind a ship, looking around.

"At this time, there are no more locals or tourists around. We'll have to be careful."

"Then, I advise being even more careful," a voice echoed from above.

Both Castiel and I simultaneously almost snapped our necks by turning around, alarmed, only to find a grinning Raphael looking down upon us.

"Are you guys on a date? It's not the appropriate place here," he whispered after looking around.

I ignored his question and frowned at him. "What the heck are those clothes you're wearing?" I asked in disgust.

"These were quite pricey. I bought them at a costume shop," Raphael answered, looking down at his dirty, torn, and holes-filled clothes, offended by my question.

"So you've been assigned to this harbor. Did you spot the guy we've been keeping tabs on?" As always, we could only count on Castiel to ask important questions.

"Oh, Boccaccio?" Raphael asked, surprised, "Nah, I'll be looking for him since he may recognize me then."

"And there is also one of your neighbors who live in the same building as us," I inserted.

"Who?" Raphael asked, his eyebrows furrowed.

"I don't know his name, but he's handsome, with slight stubble, maybe a few years older than us, and wore all black," I described. Castiel sighed beside me, tugging me back.

"We need to get going, or else we'll be caught."

"And I need to get back to my job. It's my first day here, after all," Raphael nodded and waved at us as we continued our little walk.

It was tiring, being pulled by Castiel to hide behind ships and containers every minute. I almost broke off running, yelling,' Where are the dope cookies? '

"Don't look, they are on that white and blue ship, ten meters away," Castiel informed me as we hid behind the red containers that were big enough for us to stand normally instead of crouching on the ground wet with some splashes of dirty seawater.

"So, we follow in?" I whispered.

Instead of replying, Castiel pushed me to the other corner of the container just in time as some men passed by, carrying some boxes. I watched from the corner as they emptied the ship while loading the black van; even my phone got a nice shot of them.

I saw most of the men heading to the next ship and nudged Castiel, pointing to the ship where no one was on board. He didn't say anything and, instead, waited.

After a few minutes, he clutched my hand again and dragged me, running on the gangplank, landing on the ship with a soft thud. We ran across the deck to the other side, crouching behind a barrel.

"We need to get to the hold," Castiel whispered.

"Should we split?" I mumbled back.

"No way in hell. I'm not leaving you anywhere alone," he said harshly.

"How romantic of you to say that," I retorted sarcastically.

"The path to the lower area must be near the quarterdeck; let's move," Castiel said.

Voices coming from where we were headed us retract in our steps. Searching for a hiding place, I looked at the cabin beside me. I tried opening the door, and luckily it did. I slid in swiftly, tugging Castiel along.

I pinched my nose as the smell hit me, wanting to step out as swiftly as I got in. The stench of fish hit me hard in the nose, giving me a nauseous feeling. I definitely chose the wrong room.

Castiel pushed me deeper in; the voices were getting louder. We waited silently in case they entered, but slowly, their voices faded until the silence reigned again.

"Let's get out. It's better being stuck in the dungeons than in this room," I exclaimed. But Castiel did not move. Instead, he was examining the crates. I never pegged him to be such an avid fish lover.

"What are you doing? We need to get out!" I hissed.

"The boxes at the back are not fish," he replied instead.

I approached him, looking around as well. I stuck my nose closer to the crate he was examining. Surprisingly, it didn't smell strong compared to the stench in the air. Castiel grabbed both sides of the crate and shook it. The sound of objects scuffling against each other was heard.

Something smelled fishy, no pun intended.

"Let's search the room for the crates that do not smell like fish," Castiel declared, moving to the other crater.

I shrugged and checked on the side of the room. I poked the suspicious boxes and cases around because I did not have the strength to move them.

The door slammed open just as I was checking the small containers in the left corner. I froze in place as a gruff voice echoed in the room.

"Abbiamo bisogno di tutte le casse di pesce trasferite in un'altra stanza."

I heard some footsteps approaching as they started moving the front crates away. I ducked down as my head almost got exposed when the crate covering me got moved.

"Perche c'e un buco in questo?" One of the men demanded sharply.

There was some hassle around, followed by the movement of containers. Something must have been wrong with those as the men examined the crates. Right in time, a squeak echoed in the room, halting what the men were doing. I wished to take a peek to see what was going on, but the grey thing that scurried past me told me enough.

"Sono sempre quei fottuti ratti," one of the men grunted.

After a few seconds, the men took some crates and moved out. As soon as the door closed, Castiel appeared beside me. "We have to go now. They'll carry out their usual night patrol soon," he whispered.

We bolted out of the cabin, and I took a deep breath of fresh air. We hid near the quarterdeck, and as soon as the men entered the cabin again, we ran to the main deck and jumped off the ship.

Halfway through our run, we got held up by an old man glaring at us. He asked us a question, which seemed to mean what we were doing here. I glanced at Castiel and back at the man. "Sorry?" I cocked my head in confusion.

"I asked, 'What are you doing here?'" he responded with impatience.

"We are actually on our honeymoon here, staying at the Del Luna Hotel. We were searching for a yacht to rent for some time," Castiel swiftly replied.

I looked at him. Really now? His hand pressed mine as a warning.

I gave the fakest lovely smile I could produce to the old man, leaning towards Castiel, my other hand clutching his arm with fluttering eyes. I hoped I was able to project the lovey-dovey expression well.

"At this time?" the old man grumbled, his expression full of doubts.

"Well, you know, it's always more romantic at night," I said, adding a sweet chuckle afterward for impact.

"There are yachts on the other end of the harbor, and no one is allowed here at this time. Hurry along," the man gestured for us to go away.

"Thank you," Castiel nodded, and before I could ask why no one was allowed, the man walked away.

We continued sprinting through the harbor path and walked casually in the more lighted areas. Hurried footsteps echoed behind us, and before I could turn around, a hand slung over my shoulders. A grimace came onto my face once the smell reached my nose. I pushed the hand away and glared at the culprit, standing a step away.

"I was hoping you guys wouldn't leave without me," Raphael grinned.

"I wish we could have left without you," Castiel stated as we arrived at the car, away from suspicious eyes.

"Wait," I said before Raphael could get in. I reached for the towel at the back and laid it on the backseat. "There you go, no direct contact with the car, please,"

I gestured for him to enter. He rolled his eyes at me and ruffled my hair when he entered. I took a deep breath to calm myself and got in the passenger seat.

"I need a grand shower after all those smells I came in contact with. As for you, did they throw you in the bin by any chance?" I muttered at Raphael, glancing back at his clothes, soiled and some parts wet.

"The state of the ships is like literal bins. That's the worst job I have ever attempted. A rat even walked on my feet while it ran away when I was moving a container," he groaned. I shuddered at the thought of this almost happening to me.

"Take a thorough shower once we arrive," I commented.

"Don't think I'm the only one that smells," he retorted. "Yours overpowers mine," I mocked him, rolling my eyes.

And that's how our polite exchange continued till we reached back to the apartment.

As we stepped foot there, I dashed to the bathroom before Castiel could do so. I spent a long time in there, making sure to get rid of the awful smell. I even sprayed some perfume around. After finishing, I sprawled on the sofa, switching on the TV.

I almost dozed off when someone nudged me. I opened one eye.

"Move," Castiel said.

"What are these?" I pointed to the three other sofa chairs in the room.

"My apartment. My choice. So move."

I let my legs fall on the ground as Castiel took his place beside me. I rolled my legs around to hang on the sofa's edge as I dozed off again.

Some mumbles and whispers, after a while, brought me back from my nap. As soon as I opened my eyes, I shot up straight when I saw Shooky and Raphael sitting across from me.

"What are you guys discussing?" I asked drowsily. Raphael shushed me and continued speaking. I walked to my room and came back, throwing the packet on the table. Raphael stopped talking, eyeing the packet with great curiosity. Castiel grabbed the packet, analyzing it.

"Where did you get that?" Shooky's gruffly voice resounded.

"The ship," I shrugged. Three pairs of glares were thrown at me.

"Relax," I held up my hands in defense, "a rat took the blame for it."

They still stared at me.

"I'm going to sleep," I muttered, heading back into my room silently.

☆☆☆

After buying a can of coke at the vending machine in the morning, I kept pacing back and forth on the ground floor as I searched about what I could do around or where I could go on my phone. Castiel announced that I was to leave tomorrow and that my papers had been arranged, so I was trying to make the most out of my one day.

Trying to meddle in the special agents' work served no use. I was drily told by an honest man that I was disrupting their work, so I backed off with no arguments.

Most of the guys left for an urgent meeting at 5 am. That was a point to admire. Agents had to be morning people...or maybe night owls as well since their job demanded all twenty-four hours of their day.

I marched up the stairs to Castiel's apartment absentmindedly. As I made another turn, my eyes met those of the stranger. I halted in my steps, eyeing him cautiously. Should I make a run for it? But then, he did not know that I knew what he was hiding.

Acting casually, I lowered my gaze and continued walking, passing by him. But the stranger did not continue walking down the stairs. He stood still.

As I walked up, I eyed him from the corner of my eye. Finally, he sighed and spoke.

"I know you tailed me last night."

By then, I was already some steps away. I froze. I blinked a few times, processing what he said.

"And I know you went till the harbor and on the ships as well," he said. I felt his gaze on me as he turned around, though my back still faced him. I looked up the stairs; I could still run for it, or even better, I could scream.

"Don't you want to know why I led you to the harbor and I let you follow my trail?"

Okay, that was harsh; he was testing my weak point. But curiosity killed the cat. I should ignore him. But then, when did I turn head away when such secrets were revealed? They were, after all, useful information for my dear agent friends.

I turned around, keeping a stoic look.

"Who are you?" I asked again, glaring at the stranger. He looked down and sighed.

"Look, there are some things I need to say, and my identity is not the main concern," he said, taking one step toward me before I halted him with my hand.

"I can't tell you in the open like this," he pressed, glancing around.

"Last time I ran to someone for information, I got drugged and dragged here. You're practically telling me to act like that again," I said, rolling my eyes. "Okay, I understand," he nodded and turned, continuing his path downstairs. "Let's talk in the lobby. At least you'll feel safe there."

I followed behind him, still maintaining a distance between us. We marched down the stairs to the lobby, which was quite spacious. The sunlight hit through the glass doors, lighting up the place and making the cream marble floor look shiny and polished.

People constantly moved around, going in and out. Even if he wanted to do something, he would be unable to.

He directed me past the reception area, where a man was seated. Near the twin doors of the main entry were some unoccupied red velvet armchairs that surrounded a tiny table. He gestured for me to sit down on the armchair across from him.

I followed suit, sitting down. I squeezed my hands between my thighs out of habit and pursed my lips. I looked at the man anxiously, waiting for his reply.

"First of all," I started holding my finger up, "I need a name to your face."

"Luca."

"Luca?"

"Yes, Luca."

"Okay, continue. When did you first realize we were tailing you?"

"From the start," he shrugged.

I raised both eyebrows at him.

"When I got in my van with Boccaccio, I knew you saw us and were also aware of his identity. So it was a given that you'd follow us, not that the stupid one realized. Only I saw you guys."

"That does not explain why you didn't stop us at any point of the night despite being aware we were snooping around," I stated, confused, with furrowed eyebrows.

"Because my personal goal is not to stop you. Rather, it is to bring you all to that place and see what is going on." "Alright," I drawled with a blank mind. I tried to make sense of what he said. "So you were purposefully guiding us there."

"You must have realized by now how this is a whole complex system of the drug trade, not restricted only to Italy," he attested. I nodded, frowning, wondering where he was going with it. "I want to bring it down," he finished.

I stared at him dead in the eyes for a few more seconds, processing his words. He seemed uncomfortable as he shuffled in his seat.

"Should I continue, or do you need more time?" he asked.

"More time," I muttered, focusing on my thoughts as I stared at the glass table in front of me.

"Okay," I said after a deep breath. "One question. On whose side are you?"

My own.

"Eh?"

"I am not supporting any group from any side. I have always been inside the illegal system. But like I said, I have a personal goal, to be more precise, a vendetta against the people in control. That's why I want to break down the whole system."

"So you are on our side? Like the legal side?"

"Not necessarily. I need the ability to destroy the system, not in my capability but the law enforcement people."

"Then, how long have you had this supposed vendetta? And against whom? And who else knows about your goal?"

"It's been a while now against those in command like I said. Telling you the names would put you in danger. And no one knows what I've been trying to do now."

"But what about the Ita-"

"I absolutely cannot trust the Italian police force," he cut me off. "I've been involved in this long enough to know the number of people from our side that have infiltrated the legal system. If I acted as an informant, the one who would end up being locked up is me only.

That's why the justice system is so flawed and fucked up," he scoffed.

"Then, why the IOF? Why involve them?"

"Because they have already started being involved and stopped some drug deals. And they even came here, close to the foundation of the criminal organization behind those drug trades."

"And the IOF has a more compact organization, so there is less chance of being infiltrated by spies," I mused over it to myself as Luca nodded.

"So, after everything you said, how can I believe it is all true?"

Luca let out a dry chuckle. "I knew you would not believe me. I am willing to talk it over with the IOF, so I can continue what I am doing, and they remain confidential about it."

"They are not the types to listen to a suspicious stranger's demands and accept silently, but you are right in revealing everything to them. I cannot get involved since I'll be leaving-"

I looked down as I felt my phone vibrate in my pocket, indicating a message. Thinking it may be from Castiel, I took it out and checked.

Angelia 10:20

Hey, it's Angelia! Wanna meet up? I have to go abroad for another gallery expo soon, and I don't know when you're leaving, so I'd like to meet up before I go. :D

I mused over it. Since I was leaving tomorrow, today was the right time to visit her. I didn't have anything planned as, well. I texted an 'OK' back to her, asking where to meet.

Luca looked at me questioningly. I slipped my phone back into my pocket and stood up.

"So, yes, I was saying that I am leaving tomorrow, so it'd be best for you to speak to the IOF. Maybe they'll return soon. I have to go right now, though. Talk to you later," I said, with a slight smile, turning towards the door.

"Wait!" he called out. I looked back with a puzzled look.

"Look, I've already told you before, but I'll repeat it. Going anywhere alone is dangerous, especially when you have already been a target. Kidnapping and murder cases are always floating around. I don't want to find out about yet another one I could have prevented," Luca said darkly.

"It's...okay. I'm just meeting with a friend, and I will be near the crowded areas," I said slowly. He seemed a bit sensitive to that issue. Before I could say anything more, he shook his head and walked towards the stairs, towards his apartment. I shrugged and walked out, checking Angelia's second message about the location.

☆☆☆

I let out a heavy sigh. "I don't feel that good walking right after a meal. I can barely walk."

Angelia chuckled beside me, making small steps as she walked to match my pace. We had lunch after arriving at the location she sent me, a very busy restaurant near a small lake. Due to many customers coming, we had to leave after eating, and Angelia insisted that a walk by Campelli lake was necessary.

We walked on the smooth, polished, grey pebblestones, some feet from the lake. I took a few photos of the lake, which glimmered and twinkled under the blue, sunlit skies. I heard a paddling of ducks quacking as they disappeared behind the reedbeds before I could get a photo of them.

My attention returned to the blue sky, free of any wandering clouds. Some small birds and dragonflies roamed some meters above the mirrored image of the sky. The slight breeze beside the lake kept me cool, despite the midday sun beaming high above.

I paused the walk, grabbing a flat pebble as I launched it across the lake. I always had to try this each time I got the chance.

Plop!

It went down in one hit. Angelia muffled a laugh behind my back.

"Nevermind, I was never good at it anyway," I mumbled.

We marched for a while longer, and as I glanced behind, the restaurant was already out of sight. We must have had a long walk. I didn't even notice time passing by. Maybe we should be heading back now.

As I was about to speak, I saw three men approaching from some distance. I thought they were some random fishermen or locals passing by, but Angelia slowed in her steps beside me. Her eyes widened at the sight of those men, and she stopped walking.

"Is something wrong?" I asked, glancing between the men and her. She remained silent and stared ahead with a blank expression.

The men were now some feet away and paused in their steps. The men seemed to be in their fifties, with long grey beards. They had bandanas around their heads and wore sunglasses. They looked like a typical biker gang.

The man in the middle stood in front of Angelia. I felt his intimidating glare through the sunglasses. I heard him gruffly muttering something. I cocked my head at Angelia, gauging her reaction. Her eyes narrowed as she answered back in a snappy voice.

I could not understand anything, but there was a dangerous vibe around. I placed one leg behind, almost turning back, ready to run.

"Should we go-?" I started but got cut off by the man yelling something as the two other men came forward, grabbing Angelia's hands and dragging her away.

I turned back, walking towards them, and took hold of Angelia's arm, holding her back.

"Wait, wait! You cannot do this!" I breathed out, panicked.

The men looked at each other. They did not seem to have understood a word of what I said. They shrugged and continued dragging a struggling Angelia with them.

I huffed, looked around, and took a deep breath, readying myself.

"HELP! HELP ME!" I yelled, turning back, ready to run.

As I took another breath to yell, one of the men ran from behind me, grabbed my shirt from behind, tugging me down on the ground. I flinched as my head hit the pebbles.

I tried to get up by throwing a punch to distract the man, who kept his sweaty hand on my mouth. He swiftly grabbed my hand as I heard some voices behind me. I heard the voice of a young man as well. Did someone hear me and come to our rescue?

I tried lifting my head, but the man slammed me back down, yelling something which sounded like an instruction. I couldn't hear anything as my heartbeats drummed against my ribcage.

Someone came into my line of sight, blocking the sun and forming a shadow over me as I squinted my eyes at him. Before I could speak, he handed a cloth to the old man, who took it and pressed it over my face. I reached out to stop him, but I felt someone else holding back my hands.

Slowly, after a few seconds, I felt my struggling hands weaken. A heavy feeling consumed me as my eyes closed. Someone picked me up and started walking. All voices faded in the background, and only two words came into my mind.

Not. Again.

✫ ✫ ✫

My head had repeatedly hit the moving floor. Wait, why was the floor moving again? Oh, right! They had thrown my unconscious body at the back of a van. With each bump they ran on, I took a hit.

I couldn't even move because I couldn't risk more damage being done to me. And my eyes felt like they had been tightly shut against my will. I soon drifted back into a temporary slumber.

I regained consciousness when I felt myself getting dumped on some cold ground. As the footsteps faded away slowly, I sat up with a groan. That's what we get when we try to help people.

My gaze wandered around, surveying the bland room. It was very small, almost like a cage. Grey concrete walls surrounded me, with a brown panel door to the room's left. I looked up at the small lighting I was getting from the window and realized that it was only a small hopper window.

Instinctively, I reached outside of the hopper with my hands and felt a soft texture on my hands. Was that grass? I jumped up a few times to catch a glimpse of where I was and realized that the room I was holding was below ground level.

Crouching down, I took a deep breath as I looked around the empty room again. Where was Angelia, and what did they do to her? And why did she get into trouble with them to start with?

The light that filled the room became dim, showing signs of the setting sun. Castiel and everyone else must have returned to their apartments. I wondered if they knew that I had gone missing. I reached down, patting my back pocket.

There was no sign of my phone. I hit my head back against the wall in irritation. I must have either dropped it earlier, or those goons took it. I screeched in annoyance-

Wait...

I looked down at my wrist and gaped. That was it!

I breathed in relief as I took out my watch. Well, not really 'my' watch. I borrowed Castiel's recording watch, just in case. Naples proved to be a city where all unexpected things happened. I held back a grin as I activated the GPS Tracker. The invention of technology was always a blessing.

I halted in my movements when I heard the sound of shoes clicking on the ground as someone approached. I stood up, alarmed. My gaze returned to the watch. They would find out what it was if their eyes fell on this.

The jingling of keys echoed in the room as someone unlocked the door. As quick as I could, I lightly jumped, throwing the watch out of the hopper, and sat down. Just in time to see the door opening, with a man and a woman coming in.

I masked my startled face behind an aloof expression, hoping they didn't notice anything.

The woman looked too old to act gothic. I'd say she was in her late thirties, but she wore a tight corset with fishnet and leather gloves. Her hair was black, with a small streak of blue. She seemed like a wannabe gangster and did not intimidate me. The man was one of the three men I had met earlier.

I glanced between both, wondering what they wanted. The woman approached me, crouching down to my level.

"What?" I snapped, frowning at her.

She did not look back at me and instead searched around, patting my pockets. The man came forward and pulled me to stand by my arm. I pushed him away, but he wouldn't move. The woman shook her head at him. I knew what they were searching for, but I frowned harder, hiding my relief. My phone must have fallen back where they had taken me.

Taking the opportunity, I grabbed the beard of the oldie and pulled hard. His grasp around my arm loosened as he groaned, and I pushed him away.

I dashed to the open door. I hoped there would not be many people around that would be in my way. I needed to find Angelia first, hoping she was not harmed.

As I turned around the door, someone coming in took me by the arm and flung me back inside. My butts hit the ground with full force.

"Cosa stai facendo? Ti ho detto di legarla," the soft but cold voice stated.

My words got stuck down my throat as I looked up with frozen eyes at the familiar face, stunned. I felt my breath knocked out of my lungs.

"Angelia?" I asked, my voice coming out as a whisper. "Angelia? What is going on?"

I frowned in confusion, meeting her cold stare. My eyes trailed down at her black pantsuit and her black suede boots. Her inky black hair was slicked back.

That seemed like an unusual look on her.

My confusion quickly dissipated or increased when a replica of the same person entered. The real Angelia eyed me nervously and glanced back at the duplicate. I was sure I was not seeing double because it was easy to differentiate between them. The duplicate wore all black while Angelia was still wearing her white dress from earlier.

Angelia's duplicate rolled her eyes at her and fixed her glare on the man and woman behind me.

"Sei sordo? Ti avevo detto di legarla. Adesso!" she snapped at them.

The old man bowed his head and scurried out, with the woman following his trail, probably searching for the needed materials.

The look-alike turned back to Angelia, whispering something in a harsh tone. She gave me a side glance and smirked at me. What was the deal with her?

She pushed Angelia sideways, making her stumble some steps away, and left without any more words. Oof, I felt the love.

Silence filled the room again. My hard gaze fell on Angelia, who was staring at the floor, resigned. She had the guts to remain quiet after whatever happened today. I felt a burning rage threatening to erupt inside of me. Most especially, at myself, for falling into this pit of deception.

"Look, I'm sorry. I didn't know this would happen," she finally said, releasing a frustrated sigh.

"You did all this on purpose, right?" I let out a dry laugh and focused on her, "Meeting me, talking to me, befriending me. In the end, you're double-faced like everyone else." I shook my head in disappointment.

"I'll explain," she said, taking a deep breath.

"Oh, you better. First of all, tell me, who is that bitch?"

"Violetta. My twin."

"Both of you are quite similar. Of course, I don't mean your appearance but your character instead," I sneered.

"Let me explain before you assume," Angelia interrupted sharply, clenching her fists in annoyance.

"Seeing my current situation, my assumption is right, irrespective of the excuses you'll try throwing at me. I'll hold you responsible if anything happens to me," I retorted.

"Do you know who my family is?" Angelia asked seriously.

I scoffed, rolling my eyes. "Who else but a bunch of bit-" "Verdino. Verdino is my surname."

I froze, gaping as the name rolled out of her mouth, echoing in the empty room and my blank mind. A stillness reigned about as I processed what she said.

"As I was saying, a bunch of bitches," I completed, staring at her in what must have seemed a judgemental way.

"You're partly right in thinking so. Violetta is the biggest one among us, too," Angelia shrugged. I opened my mouth to bring up yet another remark when she stopped me with her palm.

"Let me explain everything first. I only have time until someone returns."

"Oh, of course. But I have all the time. After all, it seems I'll be here for a while or forever, thanks to someone," I muttered. Angelia ignored me and started talking, pressing her hands together as she leaned against the wall.

"First of all, I have to rectify many of your assumptions. I am a Verdino, but I was never a part of any criminal activities linked with the family." Should I tell her that kidnapping was very much illegal and criminal activity?

"And I admit, I did approach you because of Violetta. But that's only because she threatened me.

She must have made you her target for a while when she made Alessio bring you to Italy-"

"Wait, what?" I gasped at the revelation.

"Yes, she told me that it was Alessio-"

"No, no, you mean Alessio is not the 'Boss'?"

Angelia glanced at the door and back at me, gesturing at me to lower my voice. "Look, this is usually kept a secret, but since I'm already telling you everything-"

"Which seems to send me the message that I won't get out alive," I gulped.

"No! Look, I don't know what her plans are. I didn't even know that she was going to kidnap you. She only told me to keep an eye on you, suspecting that you knew something. But now I feel she wants to use you as bait."

I clutched my head in frustration. "Why do you listen to her if you are not part of all this shambles?" "If you compare us, Violetta has a whole organization and contacts from different fields behind her. I have no one. The last time I refused to comply with her demands, she got me into a scandal about supposedly stealing someone else's painting and sent rumors circulating that most of my works were imitations. I had trouble getting out of that and even had to take a break. I have my career; she can destroy it with a finger snap."

"So you can't do anything but exchange your career's safety with someone's life. I will be kept here for days, months, or years but you will resume your normal life tomorrow. Have you no conscience at all?" She pursed her lips, looking around as her eyes got teary. She let out an irritated groan and came forward, crouching down, and grabbed my hands.

"Look, I am really sorry. I had warmed up to you already, and I did not know Violetta would make such a move. All she demanded me to do was relay any suspicious detail, and I told her that you knew nothing and was even going to return to London. But she's crazy and unpredictable!"

"Okay, I don't have anything else to say," I mumbled, with no power left to argue back.

Angelia's hands tightened around mine. She released my hands, standing up just in time as two men entered the room. One of them wordlessly walked over, pulling both my hands forward, and the other tightened a rope around my wrists. I glared at those men. Why tie me when I was already caged?

"I'm sure the IOF will be able to help you-"

I cut her off as my legs were also being tied. "They must be already aware that I disappeared, and I am sure they will search for me. But how do you know they'll find me on time? As you said, your sister is unpredictable, and you are unaware of her plans. Maybe this is the last time you see me, alive at least."

Angelia remained silent. The two men stood up and said something to her, probably saying it was time to go. I rolled my eyes at her.

"Just leave. Go on with your normal life, continue living in constant fear for your career and baiting other victims into your deceptive trap," I shrugged, looking nonchalantly, though I felt nothing as such on the inside.

"I'll do my best to help you in any way I can. I do not want such a burden on my shoulders."

"Will you, now?" I chuckled dryly.

"I promise."

"If you want to help me most slightly, then pass a message to the IOF telling them I have the watch."

She looked confused but nodded.

I didn't look at her as she turned around, leaving. I waited for the door to my freedom close, leaving me in complete darkness and hopelessness. I leaned against the wall, my head facing the grey ceiling. I brought my knees up, putting my tied wrists around them. The silence grew deeper, and I could hear the steady rhythm of my heartbeats.

Tears filled my eyes, threatening to overflow. I let out a shaky breath and lifted my head, trying to contain them. It must have been the cold wind of the night. I looked up and saw that they closed the small window as well, blocking even the slightest night breeze or light from reaching me.

At least I was able to put the watch out. I hoped that whatever was spoken here was able to reach outside. At this point, I doubted if it was even important anymore or would serve any use.

What would they do to me? Transport me to another place or country even? Just hold me, hostage here? Drug me yet again? Beat me? Or the worst...kill me and send me to waste disposal like all the others?

Even outside the door, there was no movement. No one must have been guarding this room, considering that there was no chance of me being able to escape. My eyes felt heavy, and my body felt exhausted. They tied my hands and legs a bit too tight; I felt the blood flow slowing down. I closed my eyes for a while. The empty room cooled off quickly, and the wall sent a chilly sensation down my back, my light shirt doing nothing to keep off the cold.

After a few hours, I opened my eyes again and felt heavy footsteps resounding across the room from outside. I thought someone was going to enter, but they passed by hurriedly. After a few seconds, I heard someone else passing by, their footsteps suggesting that they were running. Someone else was returning from the opposite direction.

Some people speaking in a hushed, agitated tone reached my attentive ears. I wanted to stand up, but the rope around my ankles stopped me. Instead, I rolled over to the door. My ears were glued to the door, waiting to know what the distress was.

I did not hear a word as my body rolled out of the room when someone opened the door. My startled eyes met that of a young guy who did not seem surprised. Instead, he reached for a cloth in his pocket and approached my face.

"Wait! W-what is going on? Stop!" I tried kicking around, but my tied feet made me look like a dying fish flopping out of the water. The young guy covered my eyes, and voices were thrown around as I heard more stomping around. My voice was muffled by a cloth forced into my mouth.

I snapped my head side to side, confused. If it weren't for the thing blocking my mouth, I would have screamed when I felt myself thrown on a sturdy shoulder, hitting my stomach along the way.

After a few seconds, I found myself thrown in what seemed to be yet another van. They are transporting me to another place, as I feared. I felt the van rumbling to life, and some men were talking. It was frustrating to be held hostage in a foreign land. Some words in their speech made me freeze; I was sure they said 'IOF' a few times. Were they panicking because of the IOF? Did the GPS Tracker work?

I wished I could be happy. But the moving van told me otherwise.

☆☆☆

Castiel's perspective

"Her phone keeps ringing, but she is not picking up."

"Call again," I said, throwing my suit jacket on the sofa and glaring at Raphael.

"Don't look at me like that. I've done nothing wrong," he muttered as he called Haelyn for the hundredth time again.

"It's useless calling again and- Hello? Who is this? What do you mean? Okay, I'll send you the address."

I raised an eyebrow at him. "A woman picked up the phone and said she'll bring it to us. She didn't say anything more."

A groan left my mouth before I could stop it. I clenched and unclenched my fists to stop the headache. Returning to an empty apartment nowadays always indicates trouble. I grabbed my suit jacket again.

"Should I inform the others?" Raphael's worried voice only increased the tension. I turned to him and was about to speak when the doorbell rang.

"Must be one of them," Raphael muttered, walking to the door and opening it. I frowned at the appearance of the stranger I tailed yesterday. What was he doing at my door? I went to Raphael's side and spoke, "Is there something you need?"

The man kept his face composed but I saw a hint of a surprised look. "Haelyn didn't tell you anything?" he asked, cocking his head.

Raphael and I exchanged looks. He signified a threat. And if he talked to Haelyn, something dangerous must have occurred, especially if Haelyn did not get to tell us about it.

"Come in," I said, restraining my emotions and keeping a stoic look. I turned to Raphael. "Call Claudius and Lucio."

I led the man to my living room, analyzing him closely. He looked quite familiar, other than being a face I saw around.

"Get to the point. Do you have any idea where Haelyn is?"

He looked confused at the abrupt question. "You mean she has not returned yet? I talked to her a few hours ago."

"Where has she- Wait, just say what you have come here for first," I snapped.

He started talking, and Claudius and Lucio joined us in the middle of his explanation. He went over the details of what he did, and I was surprised that he was revealing all this in front of people who could arrest him anytime.

"And as I told Haelyn that I am willing to reveal everything to you, she got a message and left. She said she was meeting up with a friend," he finished.

"There is a woman Miss Haelyn met a few times," Claudius inserted.

Another ring of the doorbell echoed. Raphael, already standing, walked to the door, and opened it. I heard an anxious female voice saying something. Before I could get up, a young woman entered the room. I recognized Haelyn's phone in her hand.

"Look, you need to-"

She stopped in her sentence, gaping at the man who looked as startled as herself.

"Angie!"

Luca! What are you doing here?

I could ask the same of you!

"That's the woman Haelyn used to meet," Claudius quipped amidst the confusion.

"Do you have something to do with her disappearance?" I asked, my voice coming out like a snarl directed at her.

The woman gulped at the stares she was receiving, and I saw clear guilt on her face. She turned to the man, Luca, in an agitated manner.

"I'm sorry, really sorry. Violetta took her!"

This time, Luca stood up, looking shocked and angry. "Guys, I'm not understanding anything and you're going too fast. Can someone explain?" Raphael muttered, staring at us with wide, confused eyes.

"Violetta is the one who is behind Haelyn's disappearance," Luca said, sighing.

"And who is she?" Raphael asked again.

"Our sister," both Luca and the woman echoed.

"So, you're four siblings in total?" Raphael confirmed. I paced restlessly around the room as they asked the man, Luca, about his family.

"Yes, Alessio is 29 years old, a year older than Angelia and Violetta. I'm the youngest, being 26 years old." "So your sister, Violetta, is the one controlling everything? Not Alessio? But how come?" Claudius asked, confused.

"Yes-"

"Can we discuss that later?" I interrupted.

"What?" Raphael asked, frowning.

"I believe we have someone to save right now. Discussion and questions are not the priorities," I said, trying hard to keep my calm. Turning to the woman, Angelia, I asked, "Where is she?"

The woman played with her fingers, showing her nervousness as she avoided my glare. "I'm not good with directions," she mumbled.

Before I could say something, she held up her hand. "B-but she said something! She told me to pass on the message that she had the watch. I don't know what she meant, though."

I caught the eye of Raphael, his hand searching around in the small drawer next to the sofa. Raphael nodded at me in confirmation and took out his phone. I ran my fingers through my hair, slightly messing it with frustration, and walked to Raphael's side.

"If she said that, she must have turned on the Tracker. It won't be hard to find her then," Lucio commented as he stood up. "I'll call some of the guys to go and inform Mr. Ford of the situation as well," he hurried out.

"Do we need to hurry there without a plan right away? Wherever she's held, maybe she will be there for a while," Luca inserted.

"We cannot be sure about that, and you know how careful Violetta is due to her constantly feeling anxious. The place where they are seems normal, in the middle of a peaceful neighborhood. I don't think she'd risk doing anything there. I feel it is only a temporary place to keep Haelyn," Angelia quipped in.

"It must be a place for smooth transit, then. They won't stay there for long," I nodded as Raphael worked on tracking the location. The faster we get there, the higher the chance of getting her back.

I tapped Raphael on the shoulder, motioning him to get up, as Lucio popped in again.

"We're ready to go. I arranged for two cars. You got the location?" Lucio asked Raphael as we all followed him out.

"Yeah, I don't know where it is, but it seems two hours away, uptown. We'll find out the exact location the closer we are," Raphael said.

"Can we come along?"

Castiel turned around to face the nervous-looking woman, raising an eyebrow.

"This is a hostage rescue and can be dangerous. So, we cannot take such a risk," Lucio said.

Really? She was the one who led Haelyn into that trap and now wanted to play savior. Why does no one use their brain when needed?

"Right. We'll wait here instead," Luca said, drawing his sister back by the shoulders.

Ignoring them, I marched to the first car and entered the driver's place. The rest of the men filled in right after, with Raphael sitting in the passenger seat with his mobile in hand.

"Lead the way," I mumbled, trying to calm my hands that were pressing hard on the steering wheel.

"Is this the place?" I peered forward, trying to make out the building in the darkness. It was a residential house with walls high enough to ensure privacy.

"But does it make sense?" Claudius asked from behind. "This is the residential area where so many people live."

"This is the uptown area, what do you expect? They are the ones that hide more things. Some months ago, a socialite in this area had been arrested because he was using his house to keep teenage girls as prostitutes and selling them to business partners. Your neighbor does not care what goes on about here," Lucio grunted and got out.

We all followed, and I approached the front gate. It was 10 pm, and most houses still had some lights on. But this house bathed in the darkness of the night. It felt deserted and soulless, an ominous silence floating along with the breeze.

"Let's ring the doorbell instead of just breaking in, just in case," Raphael whispered and clicked the button. We waited in silence as a buzzer alarm resounded somewhere inside. No sign of movement was spotted anywhere from inside.

My annoyance kept rising over time. The gnawing thought that we were too late persisted in my mind, despite my best efforts to ignore it.

"Let's go in," I declared, reaching for the gate bars. "Oh, and Raphael, activate the alarm sound on the watch."

With a tight grip, I leaped over the gate, landing with a soft thud. I turned on my phone's flashlight to walk around the spacious lawn. Soft, crumbling sounds of dry leaves resounded under my feet.

The other guys soon followed, faint thuds echoing one after another behind him. Lucio came forward and eyed the one-story house with scrutiny.

"We should go around quietly. There is no sign of their vehicles around, nor is there any sight of them. There is a high probability they have already left. We should not make any noise that will cause a scene," Lucio whispered, audible enough for everyone to hear.

The rest of the men passed by me and rushed to surround the house. Raphael nudged me from behind, interrupting my thoughts. "Let's follow the alarm. I can hear it from a distance," Raphael said, walking forward.

Our boots brushed against the untamed grass, making a rustling sound with our quick movements. The beeping sound echoed louder in the quietness as we moved closer to the back of the house. Finally, I spotted the red light of the watch, which was usually turned on along with the alarm.

I dropped to one knee, picked up the watch, and turned off the alarm. My eyes immediately went onto the closed holler window. Oh, so the house had a basement floor.

Raphael took the watch from his hands, analyzing it. "She had turned on the recorder as well.

Its time is limited to five hours; it must have turned off after that," he said as he looked at me.

Our eyes snapped to the window, which was being pushed open. We stepped back, peering in. Our eyes met that of Claudius, who saw the watch in Raphael's hand.

"The house was left unlocked. No one in."

My expression hardened, trying hard not to curse. I stood up.

"Then, everyone meets at the front," I said through clenched teeth. Turned around, I rushed to the front, with Raphael following behind.

Damian was at the front gate, one hand on the hip and the other holding his phone as he was talking. The others were looking around for any clue with torches in their hands.

Damian ended the call after a few seconds and turned to Raphael and me. "The house was left untouched for a while, and all furniture was covered. The basement, however, seems less dusty and more empty. I called back at the office, asking for information about who owns this house. It'll take a while to find out," he explained.

I nodded and turned to face the other approaching men. "Half of us should check the neighborhood's parameters in case they recently left. And find out if there are any surveillance cameras along the road. There seems to be none here," my toneless voice resounded.

Raphael handed the watch back to me and called some guys over with him. They got in the second car and left. Lucio signaled the other guys to return, and we filled the first car.

After two long hours, we arrived at their apartment at 2 am. I got out last, after parking. When I entered the building, and I noticed Luca and Angelia on the way, talking to Raphael. Turning to the elevator, I walked away, unable to talk to anyone.

I tiredly sat on my bed back in my apartment and reached for my phone. There was someone I urgently had to inform, though. I scrolled through my contacts, resting my thumb on the name of Mr. Carter. I sighed as I anxiously clicked on the name.

☆☆☆

At 5 am, most of the town was still asleep. Except for the special agents gathered in the small office. The windows were left open to allow chilled air into the stuffy room. But it didn't help in cooling down the tension.

"I called the headquarters to inform them about the issue. They'll send a hostage rescue team soon," Mr. Ford announced.

"We could take care of it, though," Raphael muttered.

Sadly, it reached Mr. Ford's ears.

"You guys are specialized as field agents, and most of your undercover operations did not include rescuing a hostage. But of course, you will assist and help in any way that you can," Mr. Ford said, eyeing Raphael, whose eyes were cast down.

"Meanwhile, maybe Luca could shed some light on this situation about his sister."

We all turned to the outsider of the meeting, sitting at the end of the table. Luca had sent his guilt-ridden and worried sister back to her apartment and proposed to help the agents by providing information. So, he ended up being the center of attention for the meeting, or the center of information, to be more specific.

I had scrutinized him for a while, long enough to make Luca feel uneasy in his seat. I was wondering to what extent he could be trusted. Luca was a Verdino, after all.

Luca leaned forward so that everyone could see him. He cleared his throat and clasped his hands together. "I am willing to provide any information I know about your questions. But I must admit that I would not know the real details since I had kept my distance from the main organization."

"A clear background information on your sister, Violetta, would be good," Lucio inserted.

"Yes! How could we never know about her if she has always been involved in the mafia? Like, for Alessio, we knew about him. But how come...," Raphael drawled off as Luca sighed.

"This is a long story. But to cut it short, Alessio was exposed to everyone as Enzo Verdino's son. Though Violetta did operate in the underground network, she got ignored a lot by Enzo, who never revealed to anyone that she was his daughter."

"Why?" Raphael asked, leaning on one arm, listening intensely.

"Well...you could say that sex discrimination is an issue in all fields of work," Luca shrugged. "Enzo concentrated more on my brother, Alessio, who was the one supposed to take charge after him." "Why is he not the leader, then?" Raphael asked again. "Seven years ago, Violetta disappeared for some months, almost a year. Enzo did not care about this fact. After all, his other children were just another among his petty workers," Luca laughed bitterly. "But karma hit him later with Violetta's reappearance." "Why?" Raphael asked with wide eyes. He was too into the story. I kicked his leg as a warning to shut up. Raphael reclined silently in his seat with his mouth shut.

"Violetta had stormed into one of Enzo's meetings with his important allies, taking them by surprise and shooting them all, with the help of some people. She was a skilled sniper since her young age."

All of us held a good amount of surprise in our facial expressions. This was not how we imagined the mafia boss to have died.

Luca continued, "All important high-status members were killed in the shootout set up by Violetta. She constructed this plan for a while, though nobody knows what she had been up to when she disappeared. The system structure became disorganized and a real mess. There was no one to take the lead."

"And that's when the organization went on low profile?" Mr. Ford asked.

"Not exactly. Most members left and joined other gangs and such. The group that Violetta controls right now is made entirely by her; very few are from the past mafia. Violetta assembled some trusted and loyal guys and founded her group. The main organization is tiny compared to the vast connections she created. Violetta is quite insecure and must have been afraid someone else would take her place; perhaps that's why."

"But you and Alessio are the most likely to take her place," Raphael interjected.

"Keep your friends close, but your enemies closer. That's what she follows. She controls us too. Despite what she says, she isn't that different from our father. She controls and tracks everything we do by keeping us close to her. Our relationship is purely business, so I have no problem finishing her off by helping you all," Luca said.

I sighed and crossed my arms. This story was quite long for a short one.

"I believe you must have had a reason for sticking around then," Lucio commented.

"Definitely," Luca nodded. "With my access around, I was able to analyze and keep track of shipments of drugs and where they go. The more information I have, the more I can hand over."

"Any useful detail then?" I asked, raising an eyebrow. "Actually, yes. The drug trade and deals are increasing more and more each day, especially internationally. We've sent several shipments to Turkey, India, Madagascar, and Thailand these past months. And that's mostly because Violetta has started selling new drugs."

"What do you mean by new drugs? Where has she acquired them from?" Mr. Ford asked gravely.

"She's been fabricating them and...testing them. From what I heard, that is. The laboratory is somewhere in Italy. When the drugs are done, they are distributed abroad. Often for further testing too. But I haven't seen for myself, so I can't give additional details on that."

"Do you at least know if test subjects were involved?" Lucio asked.

"I believe so. I heard from Alessio about some increase in deals and even getting volunteers," Luca cocked his head in thought.

Mr. Ford grabbed the laptop that Lucio had passed over to him. We stayed silent as he browsed through something, probably to confirm their doubts. He nodded to himself as he closed the laptop.

"I think we can get more information from the group we had arrested earlier. They are still going through trials, I think. We should contact the lawyers. I want to know what Dr. Sullivan received to test his victims. Argan Gregore's reports showed that he had drugs left in his system," Mr. Ford commented.

I stayed silent as my mind worked. If the drug testing lab was somewhere in Italy and Violetta was supervising it, and she took Haelyn with her, it was easy to guess where Haelyn was transported to. I clenched and unclenched my fists repeatedly to ease up on the doubts about what could happen to Haelyn. "I hope Violetta does nothing to Haelyn," Luca exclaimed, voicing my fears. "I think I should go back and investigate until I get the multiple locations where Haelyn may be held."

I considered the suggestion and spoke up before Mr. Ford. "It's a faster route to get the information, so yes, you should do so. But take Raphael along with you as a precaution. He had been working undercover around the port anyway."

The other agents looked at each other and nodded in approval. Mr. Ford also mused over the idea.

A knock at the door interrupted us. The door opened slightly, and the admin officer peaked in. "Sir, the group hostage rescue team has arrived, and there's another-" Before he could complete his sentence, his head disappeared quickly, and a hard thud was heard. The door slammed wide open, and I winced as I realized who it was.

Mr. Carter, the father of Haelyn, entered and eyed everyone with a deathly gaze. I usually remained nonchalant at anyone's stare. But Haelyn's father was someone quite intimidating, and I found myself avoiding Mr. Carter's gaze, though I was the one who had informed him.

"You. Had. One. Job."

Haelyn's perspective

My droopy eyes eyed the bottle of water thrown at me, which tugged me out of my sleep. As soon as I heard the door shut, I grabbed it and drank, emptying the whole bottle within seconds. I felt a slight burning sensation down my throat and ignored it.1 It was my third day in that canned box of a room. The room was well-lit, white everywhere, reflecting onto the metal-like walls. The red light of the little camera from above glared at me the whole day.

I kicked the bottle back to the door. I already felt the need to pee. The water calmed my stomach a bit, but I wished they had also given me food. During the past two days, someone brought me to water and guided me to the toilet only once a day. The toilet seemed the most common place here, not that I've seen much of the place. I was thrown inside the solitary cell blindfolded the moment we arrived there.

I only made a journey to the toilet twice, and there was no sight of any other person, not even my buttshit kidnapper. It wasn't like I wanted to see her, but I wondered why I was being kept in a cell for such a long time. Deep inside, I felt grateful because her giving me attention would only mean something bad.

I hoped she continued ignoring me until rescue came, which I hoped they did.

After a while of lying around, I glanced at the opening door. A man, who seemed to be in his forties, approached me with handcuffs. I backed off against the wall and realized how useless my actions were. Where could I even escape? The man silently put the handcuffs around my wrists and dragged me up.

I followed along, with stiff legs, down the corridor. My eyes focused on the similar rooms aligned on both sides of the corridor. Were there people in those cells too?

The white, spacious room finally came into my sight. I made a grimace as I saw the devil herself, leaning against a table with crossed hands. She was dressed more comfortably, in a black shirt and pants. Her slick black hair was tied in a ponytail. She provided a great contrast to all the white I've seen around.

My curious gaze moved around the room, or should I say the high-tech laboratory. It was quiet and as cold as a morgue. I spotted some computers and flat screens decorating the right side of the lab. Flasks, cylinders, tubes, vials, microscopes, and more flooded the front of the lab.

It seemed like those research labs in sci-fi movies, with a sinister feel. I was already expecting some maniac scientist to enter and declare that I was now his testing subject.

Violetta glanced lazily over her shoulders when she heard us approaching. She gestured to the man to bring me closer, which the man did, by almost punching me forward.

I could not understand what look to give the devil. Should I act indifferent? Or should I show my anxious feelings? Or I could laugh my way out of this mess.

My gaze went to my bare feet when I stood a foot away from her, avoiding her sadistic smile. Why did they have to take out my shoes when taking me again? "Eager?" Her cold voice resounded as she clicked her fingers on the table.

I looked away, rolling my eyes, and looked back at her. "Eager to return home? Yes." "Oh, don't look forward that much to this. I wouldn't want you to have high expectations," she chuckled.

"Cut the crap. That's delusional of you to think you'll get away with all this. Why am I here?" I breathed sharply. The clinging of the handcuffs echoed, making me more annoyed.

"You don't know who I am. You're here for me to show you what you dragged yourself into," she said, gesturing to the place with her hands.

"I'm pretty sure I was supposed to be home by yesterday. You dragged me here," I raised an eyebrow.

"Oh, come on, don't act so innocent. You kept interfering with my business even back in your country. You wanted a game to play. Aren't you glad to have found the real player? I bet you'd be satisfied to solve the puzzle, Haelyn. Maybe at the cost of your life...," Violetta trailed, walking around the table as her fingers lay on the rows of small vials.

I felt my blood grow cold and shiver. I clenched my handcuffed wrists tightly.

"By dragging me into the game, you made me a puzzle piece instead, bitch. It's the IOF who are gathering the puzzle pieces, one by one. All different pieces are meant to come together, and they'll get you eventually. Then you can bark your way into the jail," I sneered.

My bravour decreased a bit as Violetta paused, her fingers on one vial, as her cold emerald eyes paused on me. Then she released a sinister chuckle.

"Come in, Doctor," she said.

I frowned in confusion and turned around to see a man coming in. He must have been in his fifties, with little blond hair covering the back of his head. He was wearing a simple lab coat. My intuition told me that he was not Italian. My gaze fell behind him, on a young man who looked around my age. He followed the oldie silently, in a daze.

I took some steps back as the Doctor passed by me.

He walked to Violetta, giving her a light kiss. A kiss! Was he the boyfriend? I looked at the 'Doctor' up and down. Maybe he was younger than I thought.

I looked at them in disgust and turned to the guy beside me. He was looking at the floor. I flashed my hands before him, but he did not look at me. He looked like a zombie, so I carefully stepped away from him.

Violetta and the Doctor were whispering about some things and were looking at me. I looked around, looking for an escape. I found the door shut behind me. I looked back at the microscope. What if I throw that at them? It must be hard enough to knock them out.

The old man walked to the corner and switched off the light. We were thrown into pitch darkness. I heard another click, and a bright light shone on a table. The guy beside me walked over to the table and climbed on it like a robot without even being asked. What did they do to that poor guy?

The Doctor took a small vial with transparent liquid and a syringe. The liquid went up the syringe. I held my breath amidst the deadly silence. I wish I could disappear in the dark. The syringe was inserted into the man's arm. I gaped at him in the darkness. He was not even reacting.

The Doctor made the man sit up after finishing. He looked at me, or rather behind me, at the man who had accompanied me. The man walked to him. Violetta also approached, eyeing the other man with a maniac look. I stepped back little by little.

"Take this one away and let Luca in," she commanded. Luca seemed to be a familiar name around.

I felt hands grabbing me, pushing me forward as the two men left. I tried defending myself, but I got pushed onto the table. In full panic mode, I flung my free legs on both sides, one hitting Violetta's side and the other taking the Doctor by surprise right into his plunging stomach.

I would have laughed at their expressions if I were not in such a situation.

"Let's tie her legs," the Doctor hissed. Oh, he spoke English, definitely not Italian.

I tried sitting up, but I was hit in my throat, making me fall back. My handcuffed hands were dragged at the back, holding me in place.

"Stop! What the hell are you doing to me?" I screeched.

"We're just having some fun to make you comply better with plans. Luca, come here," the sarcastic voice retorted. I froze at the appearance of the Luca that I knew. He did not look at me and maintained a stoic look, handing over something.

My surprise distracted me from the quick sting up my arm. My shock seemed to have amused Violetta. "There, it wasn't that bad, was it?" She exclaimed in a fake cheerful tone.

I stayed still for a few seconds. What did they inject into me? Was something going to happen to me soon?

"Luca, take her back," she said. Luca approached me, detaching my legs and hands from the table as he made me stand up, still not looking at my face. I could bet that the first thing he'd say would be,' sorry, I didn't know this would happen.

"We'll see you again soon for another session," Violetta smirked as I walked away. If not for Luca's tight grip around me, I would have flung the microscope at her for real. I imagined her face getting flattened and crumbling in front of me. Phew, my sadistic self was showing!

As soon as we were out of that lab, I shook off Luca's hands violently from my shoulders and glared at him, huffing. I felt the need to scream my lungs out.

"Woah, chill," he said, putting his hands up.

I took a deep breath to calm myself down. "Look at me, idiot. Am I in a state to chill?" I said in a dry tone. "Let me take you back to your...room first," Luca said, glancing around.

"With pleasure," I said, rolling my eyes.

I hurried to the cell and entered. "You can go away now," I snapped at Luca as I sat on the floor. He closed the door and remained inside instead of leaving.

"Look, I wanna say-"

"What? You're sorry too?" I huffed.

"Uhm, well, not exactly. I do apologize on behalf of both of my sisters, though-"

"Wait, what sisters?" I asked, confused. Then my eyes slowly widened in realization.

"You mean...," I drawled off, staring at Luca, who nodded grimly at me. Everyone seemed to be related around here.

"Angelia informed the IOF though-" "How does it matter? I'll probably get drugged every day and left to die before they finally arrive. When they come, they'll either see my corpse or my zombie self like that guy earlier," My lower lip quivered, and I tugged on my hair in frustration. I felt overwhelmed, with a strong need to cry.

"That's why I'm here instead," Luca said, trying to reassure me.

"Yeah, indeed. You're helping in drugging me, after all. I am already feeling weird and heavy right now. Can you see my trembling hands? That shit is real!" I exclaimed.

"Do you want to know what drug it was?" he chuckled. Wow, he had the guts to laugh at my situation. "Does it even matter n-"

"Paracetamol."

"Uh?"

Luca leaned against the door to ensure he was not seen by the camera above. With a quiet laugh, he showed me the vial hidden in his pockets. I gaped with wide eyes, very surprised. "I swapped the bottles at the last moment. You're struggling around, and the darkness made it easy for me not to get noticed."

I stared at him, trying to understand. I felt relief overcoming me slowly.

"What if they hear you?" I asked fearfully, looking up at the camera.

"I checked. It's not auditory, and all rooms are soundproof."

Okay, but what are you going to do now? Can you help me escape?" I asked, hope returning.

"There is no chance of escaping. There are people everywhere around. The outside is more guarded, too," Luca sighed, shaking his head.

"Then...inform someone?"

"The IOF agents sent me as a spy. The last two days, I hopped from place to place, trying to find where you could be held. We are in Salerno right now, another port city. The shipments around here included lab equipment and drugs, so I decided to take control of the drugs sent here and got in."

I felt like there was a 'but' to his sentence and waited for him to continue.

"But I am stuck here as well," he sighed. "I didn't know that for security purposes, whoever comes here is held up for at least a week working around here to wait till the other group comes. I tried using my phone, but there seems to be no connection here."

"A week, though. Many things can happen during a week. Maybe I can put up with it. Nothing much can be done anyway," I mumbled, a sense of hopelessness enveloping me.

Luca pulled something small and black out of his pocket and put it near the door.

"After I go out, you take that and activate it. It is a Mini GPS Tracker. I'm unsure if it will work, but we can try anyway. Hide it carefully; if you get caught, I'll get doomed along with you," Luca explained.

"They can also track you by your phone," I suggested.

"Yes, but as I said, the connection is strange here. I think Violetta designed the place so that we cannot connect to the outside. Who knows, she may be keeping track of everyone's phones."

"Then, your phone is useless here. What you need is for your phone to be in the connection range," I mused. "If you send your phone outside through other vehicles going in and out. Please send a text to the IOF telling them to track your phone. They'll get it when it is in the connection range and can track our location even if it could be a bit far."

"Yeah, that may work. Anyway, I don't think they would be willing to wait for a week, especially your dad," Luca winced, rubbing the nape of his neck as if he remembered an awful memory.

"My dad?" I perked up, both eyebrows raised.

"Castiel informed him, and he took the earliest flight to Italy. He looked like a dragon breathing fire when he stormed into the office. We had quite some trouble trying to calm him down," Luca chuckled.

I smiled at my dad's typical behavior. He came off as a bit scary to some people. Then, I felt myself tearing up. What would he say if he saw the state I was in? I always dreamed of becoming successful like him in the legal field, but I was instead dragged into stupid, dangerous situations, needing a group of people to rescue me. I knew he'd do anything to save me but deep down, I hoped he wouldn't be disappointed in me.

"I'll be going now," Luca announced. "Don't let anyone doubt that you haven't been affected by the drug. We cannot risk getting caught."

I nodded at him, and he went out, closing the door. I relaxed a bit, knowing that Luca was here and that my being drugged was avoided for today. I slid to the door and grabbed the small tracker. I activated it and put it in my pants pockets.

I lifted my arm, looking at the pink spot where that oldie injected me, which slightly stung when I touched it. I leaned against the wall, sighed, and hoped it would work.

☆☆☆

Some minutes or hours passed by. The always-lit room made it difficult for me to calculate the time. To distract myself from being bored, I kept playing with the tracker.

The sound of the door unlocking made me drop it back into my pocket quickly. I eyed the man that entered. For a second, I thought Luca came back because of their uncanny resemblance. I already guessed who he might be.

His gaze fell on me with a smirk. He looked outside, gesturing for something. Very soon, a well-covered man dragged another man who looked unconscious and dropped him off at the other corner of the room.

"Sorry, we've run out of rooms. Learn to share," he casually shrugged. My eyes widened at him. I remembered his voice. He was the one who had called me ugly when I was feigning unconsciousness. That was him, Luca's brother, Alessio.

Before I could retort anything back at him, he left. I eyed the unconscious man carefully. Should I see if he was okay?

I almost stood up when the door opened again. I fell back in my place, staring at the intruder, who turned out to be Alessio again. "And be careful. Infections spread fast."

He disappeared again as I stared at the closed door in confusion. Infections? What exactly did the man have? I looked over at the unconscious man whose back was facing me. I stood up, maintaining my distance.

"Excuse me? Are you okay?" I whispered a stupid question. He did not look okay. I guessed that he had been a frequent victim of Violetta's fun hobbies. His hair looked unkempt, and he had wrinkles around his eyes. He seemed malnourished by the old, loose clothes that hung on his body. Despite my curiosity, I did not dare approach him.

I felt him move from where I stood. I instantly stepped back. The man lay on his back, and his blood-red eyes stared at the walls. His eyes became fixed, his pupils widely dilated. The man's lips were slightly blue. Something was wrong with him.

The man started shaking. And before I could say anything, he was violently convulsing on the ground as he frothed at the mouth. I gasped, clamping my mouth as I scrambled to the door. The color drained out of my face. I grabbed the handle by instinct, trying to open the door, despite knowing it was locked.

I blinked furiously, not knowing what to do. I couldn't even call the ambulance here. I felt claustrophobic all of a sudden, breaking into sweats. I hit the door and aggressively pulled onto the door handle. "Hey! Open the door! Anybody here?" I shouted, slamming on the door.

I looked back at him with glossy eyes. He remained still, showing no sign of movement. A small puddle of liquid poured out of his mouth beside his face. I felt nauseous the longer I stared at him.

I leaned against the door, knocking on it every once in a while. Shouting served to no use as I remembered that the room was soundproof. And the man was not waking up again.

After a long time staring at the door, I moved back when I heard the door unlocking. Before I could say anything, two men walked in. They were entirely covered and wore gloves. They ignored me and knelt beside the man, blocking my view. They seemed to be assessing him as they whispered and nodded at each other.

They then enveloped the man in something and lifted him. I didn't need to question them to know what happened. He was already dead. My heart slammed against my ribcage, and my breath came out uneven as he was led out. Was this how I was going to end up as well?

I thought they would lock the door as they got out, but someone else was flung inside. For a second, I thought that it would be another victim who was going to be left to die. I was even more surprised when I saw Violetta's face. Then, I realized it was Angelia. It was quite difficult to tell them apart.

I cocked my head towards the door, noticing Alessio.

"You should have thought at least once before telling on her," he clicked his tongue in fake disappointment though his tone was full of amusement.

"My decision to do so is way better than someone who follows her like a dog on a leash," Angelia sneered back.

Alessio's amused look faded instantly. His nostrils flared as his jaw tightened. He was fighting hard to keep his anger inside.

"Unlike you, I am calculating my moves. Once the right time comes, I will make that bitch regret taking my place," he said through clenched teeth.

Angelia scoffed at him. "That's not something we'll ever witness," she said, letting out a dry chuckle.

"You mean you won't witness this? Wanna know why? Because you won't be alive for long. You'll die a pathetic death as our parents did."

Before Angelia could retort back, Alessio shut the door with a bang in her face. She slammed her palms on the cold floor in irritation. As she lifted her eyes, she saw the silent audience she had, leaning against the wall.

"Oh God, Haelyn! Are you okay?" she asked, scrambling on her feet as she approached me with a worried look.

I nudged her hand off my knees. "You should worry about yourself," I muttered with a flash of irritation.

It felt wrong to be angry with her, but each time I looked at her face, it reminded me of her evil twin. And this made me more infuriated towards her.

She awkwardly cleared her throat and sat beside me in silence.

"Does Luca know you're here?" I finally asked after a long pause.

"No, I haven't been in contact with him for the last few days. He had told me to stay away so as no suspicions are thrown upon me...," she trailed off, sighing.

"How did you get caught then?"

"Violetta has people who work for her posted everywhere around the city, so we can never hide for long from her. Someone saw me taking your phone back from where it was dropped," Angelia shrugged.

"Oh, I'm sorry for causing you to end up here. Luca is also here, by the way," I chimed in.

She turned to me abruptly with a surprised look. "What? He got kidnapped too?" she almost screeched. "No, he was going from place to place trying to locate me, and when he succeeded, he also got stuck for a few days here. I'm grateful for both of you helping though it is dangerous. You two seem to get along well compared to the other toxic two," I remarked.

"Hmm, yeah.," she trailed off, probably walking down memory lane. "We were never that into the family business compared to Alessio and Violetta. Those two went out of control when our mother ran away, leaving us with that monster of a father."

"I can relate to that," I sighed. "My mother left my dad and me when I was twelve. But my dad was a much better parent than my mother could ever be."

"You were lucky to have at least one caring parent then. I had to take care of myself as well as Luca who was only eight then. Violetta always held a grudge against our mother. Before killing our father, she located my mother, who had escaped to Spain, where she remarried. Violetta killed her the instant she found her. And as Alessio said, I could really be her next kill."

I couldn't help but feel speechless at this revelation. I instinctively wrapped my arm around Angelia's shoulders to comfort her and ease the tension. At this rate, I felt like Violetta could do anything for her interests, which increased my fear of her.

"It's okay. I'm sure we'll be rescued soon," I whispered to her.

Right on time, the door opened abruptly. Our eyes shot up to our visitor.

Speaking of the devil.

☆☆☆

Castiel's perspective

"Did you get through to him?" Raphael asked.

"No," I replied for the hundredth time as I slammed my phone on the table. "I can't get through him."

"Maybe he has turned off his phone," Raphael mumbled as he walked by again.

A whole day has passed since Luca informed us about his whereabouts. He went to the other port city, Salerno, to inspect around but never called back again. The longer it took, the more my patience seemed to vanish. I had told Raphael to join Luca, but Raphael could only get through certain places with a few restrictions on who could access it.

I pressed my face into my palms and released a deep breath. My thoughts wandered to what Haelyn may be going through. Three days have passed. In many cases, this could mean that it was too late. Or it was my fears that were engulfing my brain and making me take this on a personal level rather than the professional level demanded of me.

"Hey! The GPS Tracker has been activated!" someone announced excitedly. I looked behind to see Damian on a laptop. I rushed over to take a peek, followed by the others around. My eyes darted across the screen.

"What is this?" I frowned.

"Someone is tampering with it," Damian groaned as he slammed the table with frustration. I stared at the blinking dot that kept switching locations on the map every five seconds.

"What is going on?" two voices chorused when the door opened.

I moved aside to give place to Mr. Ford and Haelyn's father as Damian explained what was happening. I looked at Mr. Carter's exhausted face and how his hope slowly disintegrated. The wrinkles around his eyes seemed to have multiplied. Searching for his daughter day and night had taken a toll on him, yet he refused to show any despair.

"The good news is that Luca knows where Haelyn is since he managed to pass the GPS Tracker to her. But the bad news is that we cannot get in contact with both of them. Luca's phone is unreachable," Raphael explained to Mr. Ford.

"Maybe it is because of the place where she's being held. Wherever it is, Violetta would make sure we cannot trace the location. If the last time we heard of Luca was when he was in Salerno, he must not have gone far to find Haelyn. We should look around there," Mr. Ford suggested, looking at Mr. Carter for confirmation.

"Lucio and some others are already at the port-"

A ting signaling a message cut through my sentence. I swiped across the screen and read the message.

Luca 7:17

No signal from where I am. Track my phone. I sent it out through a van that was going out. Also, advance with precaution.

Everyone eyed me questioningly as I stared at my phone.

"Let that be," I said, gesturing to the laptop and slipping my phone on the table for everyone to see. "Tracking his phone would be easier. If I got his message now, that means his phone is already within the signal range. We should act fast."

"On it," Raphael said and proceeded to grab the laptop.

The tapping sound of his fingers on the keyboard resounded across the room as we waited. Hope started to bloom among us.

"The vehicle is already close to the harbor. How will we track where they started from?" Raphael inquired as he turned the laptop for all of us to see.

"Tell the team near the harbor to stop the van from arriving at their destination. As soon as they are apprehended, make them turn around and show the way. Those vans transporting products rarely have more than two men," Mr. Carter responded.

"And we'll follow behind since we are further away," Mr. Ford nodded in agreement. "We cannot charge right in after getting the location, though. We'll follow the plan placed by the hostage rescue team."

"Let's go then," Mr. Carter said as he seemed to have got his energy back.

This time, I was determined to get Haelyn out of those criminals' grasp, no matter what.

Castiel's perspective

After having threatened the men in showing us the way, the hostage rescue team went ahead to survey the surroundings. We arrived a bit later and were waiting for any sign of them returning.

I felt the micro earphone in my ear buzz, taking me by surprise. I glanced around to see similar reactions.

The other team must have been trying to send a message. We waited for a few seconds. Glitching sounds resounded in my ear, and then they stopped.

"Did anyone hear what they said?" Mr. Ford asked as he took out his micro earphone and analyzed it confusedly.

I shook my head and took out my phone to call Mr. Carter, who went along with the first team, but the call wouldn't connect. As Luca said, the signal around was weird. I glanced at Mr. Ford and said, "If they are trying to say something instead of returning, it must be important. We should go and check."

Mr. Ford paced around, thinking about what to do. I looked to my right as I heard the cracking sound of branches. I recognized Ellen, a rescue team member, rushing towards us. She was breathing heavily and looked panicked. She stopped in front of us and stared at us with wide eyes.

"We need a bomb disposal team! Right now!" she breathed out.

A chorus of 'what's' echoed as her announcement surprised us. Mr. Ford, sensing the urgency in her words, regained his composure and asked her to explain the situation.

"We scouted the area and found a building deeper in. It did not seem protected or guarded, so we could easily sneak in. But we detected some time bombs attached to the fencing and connected by wires. I believe we have around thirty minutes in front of us. But whether this is enough depends on how soon the bomb disposal team can come," she exclaimed in one breath.

"Then let's not waste time. Try to contact the nearest police station and explain the situation," Mr. Ford said.

Lucio walked away with his phone, and I looked back at Ellen. "What about the people inside?

If they were the ones who planted the bombs around, they would not stay around."

"Weirdly enough, we spotted around five men outside. And we saw some movements from inside the building. They seem almost unaware of the bombs around," Ellen replied.

"Why would-"

A loud noise pierced through the air, cutting through my words. It was an explosive sound that made us take some steps back.

"I thought you said we have thirty minutes," Mr. Ford asked Ellen.

"That's what the team said. Something must have caused the bomb to detonate so soon," Ellen explained with a concerned look.

I took out my suit jacket as I paced around worriedly. Beads of sweat trickled down my back, making me more annoyed. Footsteps echoed around, and I looked up to see the group arriving.

"We've been spotted. A gunshot triggered one of the bombs, detonating it. Since wires connect all bombs, it won't be long till the others start exploding too. How much time will it take for the bomb disposal team to arrive?" the team leader, Mr. Brad, inquired while wiping sweat off his forehead.

"Soon," Lucio said, approaching us. "I've managed to reach them. They'll get here within a few minutes."

"This bomb situation was quite unexpected. It seemed like they were planning to blow down the building and destroy everything. I've put some men on the lookout around the building because that inside will try to escape soon," Mr. Brad said.

"It's the perfect opportunity to go in then," I announced.

"Are you crazy?" Raphael whispered harshly beside me.

"Think about it. The men inside don't have any choice but to prioritize their escape. Take them as they try to go. I'm sure Luca is still there. He'll help Haelyn escape," I explained.

"We're trudging on thin ice. We may be putting the hostage in dan-"

"She's in enough danger as it is," I cut off Mr. Brad. Another blast was heard, proving my point.

The noise reverberated over the quiet surroundings. Trails of smoke and dust rose above the few trees.

I heard the sirens and looked back to see a police van approaching. Three men, all dressed in full bomb suits with gas masks in hand, stepped out of the van, running towards us.

"Where is it?" one of them asked as soon as they arrived by our side. Mr. Brad pushed the gate wide open, gesturing for the team to follow. I silently started to follow them behind.

"Where are you going?" Mr. Ford asked behind me.

"What if those guys inside start to shoot? Someone should be in the defense position. We must follow behind, and as soon as they get the bombs into control, we rush inside," I replied as seriously as I could.

I turned back, my hand placed carefully over my gun, and followed them. We jogged to the area where the smoke came from. My eyes darted around for any form of attack, but I saw no one around. Deep among the trees, I spotted the white building. I turned around to see the bomb disposal team quickly cutting off the wires in between the bombs placed around.

"Is it safe to do that?" Raphael asked, approaching us.

"Cutting off the wires will prevent the bombs from going off all at once. One alone of this one would not cause much destruction," one of the team explained.

"Where is Mr. Carter, though?" Mr. Ford asked, looking around.

Instead of searching around, my gaze lingered on the building. I sighed and motioned to the house. "His daughter is held hostage only a few feet away. How could we have expected him to remain patient for so long like us?"

Mr. Ford facepalmed and took a deep breath. "Castiel...," he started.

"No worries, sir. I'll go in and check right away," I interrupted. With a firm nod, I started running ahead.

"What are you looking at? Follow him!" I heard him hiss at someone but didn't look back.

The more I ran towards the building, the more it felt suspiciously silent. I stood a few meters away and glanced at the windows, assessing the potential danger.

"Let's not rush into it, shall we? The other team entered from the front already," Raphael breathed out as he and Lucio jogged to my side.

"Are we here to eat popcorn and watch them?" I retorted back, walking to the backdoor.

"No need to get competitive," he groaned.

"Oh, I'm not," I said, nonchalantly opening the unlocked door. "Watch my back. I'm going in."

I stepped in, careful not to make any sounds. The inside was a fresh white and brightly lit by the sunlight hitting in from all windows. It looked like a normal house in a campagne. My dirty boots left trails of dust specks along the corridor as I walked.

We arrived near a staircase, and I turned to Raphael and Lucio, pointing toward it. "Should we?" I mouthed quietly to them.

"Hands up!" A random shout echoed, alerting us.

I raised the gun in my hand. I looked around and realized it was not aimed at us. There was no one around us. Some loud voices rose above the silence, and a gunshot resounded in my ears.

"It's around there," Lucio murmured, pointing to our far right. We rushed to the voices that got louder as we approached. We entered what looked like a living room in disarray with some sofas overturned. A group of men hurdled near a fallen door. My eyes met Luca's as he turned around with a panicked look. I recognized the other men who were part of the rescue team.

"What is going on? I heard a gunshot." I asked, peering at the stairs going down into darkness.

"The workers had locked the door from the inside. Mr. Carter shot at it to break the lock. He went in with some of them. There is more than one hostage," Luca explained.

"Isn't it dangerous if the members are in there? How many are there?" Lucio asked.

"We were about thirty in number here, but by now, no one must be left. We didn't know bombs had been planted around the area and the first one going off took us by surprise-" "How come no one knew about it? Does Violetta has something to do with that?" I interrupted.

"Possibly, yes. She left a few hours ago. If she did it, then it is not the first time that she tried bombing off a whole place to destroy evidence. But there is no time now. If we want to capture the members running away, we must hurry."

"If they tried escaping from down here, there must be some safe underground passage," I looked at Luca for confirmation.

"Yes, I had entered through that when I arrived. But the exit is a bit far from this area, and luckily enough, the door to the outside has a lock personally designed by Violetta, which will make them stall for a while. I can show you the way," he suggested.

"But-" I hesitated as my gaze fell down the stairs. I shook my head and recomposed myself. There was already a full team at my disposal to help around. I could not let personal feelings interrupt my job.

I nodded at Luca, and we turned around, marching out. I was instantly met with the sight of many people in police uniforms walking past, thoroughly ignoring us.

Luca slowed in his steps as he avoided looking at them, coughing awkwardly. I raised an eyebrow at him.

"I am kinda on the wanted list here," he chuckled.

"Nevermind. We'll say you're working with us," I shrugged.

I spotted Mr. Ford some feet away. "What are the police doing here?" I asked, gesturing to the Italian police, whose numbers were more than ours.

"Those who are heading in are going to drag out all those who are still inside. There are supposed to be bombs installed around the building as well. And they came to assess how dangerous the situation is since we asked for their bomb disposal team," he replied, crossing his arms, looking slightly unnerved by their appearance here.

"Then, let them handle that. We need to urgently stop the members from leaving through the underground passage's exit is a bit close by. Luca will help us. We do not have time to explain more right now," I said, cutting to the chase.

"Get in the car then," he said, hurrying to the car.

An explosion hit my ears as I followed after, holding the car door open and ready to get in. I froze as I saw the top right part of the building crumbling down. I was about to close the door and race back there when I felt Raphael push me inside. I glared at him, making him put his hands up in defense.

"Let's not be reckless. There are enough people to handle it."

I sighed and took a seat at the back along with him. Luca showed Mr. Ford the way beside him. I gazed back at the building. They better handle it.

☆☆☆

Haelyn's perspective

I sat on that useless excuse of a stool as I waited. I kept sliding off due to the rough moving motion of the yacht. Locked in a small room or kitchen of the yacht, I stared at the harbor, slowly disappearing the further we were going away. My face was sucked dry, full of desperation and tiredness. How did I go from seeing Violetta pop by in my prison cell to her dragging me on a yacht ride?

Violetta and her doctor boyfriend were above, guiding the yacht too. I couldn't guess where. I tried telling them how I found it intriguing how they were secretly running away and putting me in a car, but she slapped duct tape over my mouth too soon. I could hear their voices from up there, but they weren't clear enough over the water and motor sound.

With nothing to do, I surveyed my surroundings and opened the drawers behind me. Most of them had only some papers or magazines, nothing more interesting. As I was about to close the drawer, an object glinting among the papers made me stop. Putting both handcuffed hands in, I shoved the papers aside to get a glimpse of a pocket knife.

Placing it between my hands, I gazed at it with wide eyes. I wished that my hands were tied with ropes rather than handcuffed. The knife felt rather useless right now.

The jingling sound of keys made me drop it in my pants pocket as I sat up straight. I feigned an innocent look, gazing down at my feet.

The small door opened, and in stepped the devil. She ripped out the duct tape on my mouth, leaving a burning feeling on my face. She reached for the handcuffs, pulling my hands forward. I couldn't suppress the surprised look as Violetta unlocked it and took it off. And I was even more surprised when she held a gun at me.

"What do you-"

A padded jacket slammed in my face. I heard her cocking the gun as a warning. "Put that on," her dripping cold voice snarled.

I wordlessly put it on as fast as I could. She smirked as I finished and looked at her quizzically. A louder noise distracted me from her as I looked through the small window to spot another boat. It looked like a trawler and slowed down beside us.

My heart skipped a beat, but not in a good way. Were they transferring me?

The handcuffs slamming back around my wrists grabbed my attention back.

"Hurry!" I heard from above.

Violetta looked up and back at me. "I hope you have had a nice life so far," she smiled and patted my shoulder. I frowned at her.

Instead of dragging me out like I thought she'd do, she went out herself and closed the door again, and locked it. I sat stunned, facing the door. My eyes slowly turned to the other boat that was making a turn, leaving. From afar, I could spot Violetta and the Doctor on that boat's deck.

I knew she was not simply leaving me behind. There had to be something. Was the boat drowning?

I had to get out of here. Maybe there'll be other boats passing by since the harbor was around. I walked to the door and slammed my foot on it. I sat down right after, wincing as my toe crushed against the solid door.

I stood back up, looking around to spot an object hard enough to break the door open. Those papers would not be served of any use. My gaze stopped on the bright orange cylinder that rested at the bottom beside the table. A wicked smile came onto my face.

With my hands stuck together, I had trouble dragging the extinguisher to the door. I lifted the extinguisher, resting it slightly on my shoulders. I aimed near the handle and threw it with all my force.

I moved back as it fell and rolled towards me. I looked at the hole where the handle was and pushed the door open. I tried to steadily walk up the stairs, but the boat movement made me bump towards both sides.

As I reached the open, the fresh salty air hit my face. I jumped and looked around for the danger that I was surely in but ignorant of. The yacht was not drowning, it seemed. It was on autopilot, going right ahead, further and further away from the shore.

I put my hands on my heart, feeling the ticking sound of my heart-

Wait, what?

I looked down at my chest. That was not the ticking sound of my heart! It was a ticking machine in the jacket. What could it be?

My hands reached down to my pants as I tried to take out the pocket knife. With great difficulty, I managed to take it out. I placed it gracefully between my handcuffed hands and tore the jacket beside the ticking machine. I spotted red and green wires near the torn area. A sort of stopwatch stared back at me, with numbers blinking back at me.

19:43:181

And the numbers decreased with each second. My mouth ran dry at it. I've only seen that in movies. It couldn't be real.

The cool sea breeze did nothing to stop the beads of sweat that trickled from my forehead down my neck. I rushed to the yacht's helm, clutching it as I tried to turn it. It wouldn't budge.

The ticking sound made me panic. Looking around, all I could spot was sea, sea, and sea from all sides. The shore was like a tiny image left behind.

I grabbed the helm again, trying to make a turn. I had never been on such a yacht before, nor did I ever land myself in such a position before. What was I supposed to do to make it work?

My hand slipped from the helm as I hit the side. I groaned as something hard fell on my lap. I looked at it with wide eyes.

Oh...my...LUCK! A Marine VHF Radio!

I turned the squelch around, causing it to make a hissing sound. I adjusted it until the annoying sound stopped. Now, what should I do?

My eyes darted across the buttons, along with my trembling hands. As I fumbled with it, I tried thinking back to what I could remember. What was the emergency channel again? I pushed a random button, hoping it would be the distress button. I held onto it until the beep sound echoed, and the channel switched to Channel 16.

"Mayday! Mayd- wait, what was the boat name already?" I asked myself. I didn't read the name when I was pushed on board. I peered down the yacht to catch a glimpse of the name.

"Hello! Is there anyone? I'm reporting an emergency near Salerno's port! I'm on the boat, Orion!"

"You have now been transferred to Channel 16. Explain the nature of your emergency along with your location. Your message will be relayed to the Coast Guard vessels in radio range of your boat," a robotic voice answered.

I almost burst into tears at the message. Then, my inner wise self called out to me.

Don't be hysterical. The sooner you give your location, the sooner they'll send help. Dumbass.

"I'm on an Orion yacht, located a bit far from Salerno. There is a bomb on me. I'm repeating a BOMB. And I'm handcuffed! And there is like only fifteen minutes left till it goes off! An-and that's it, I guess. How do I send this now? Oh- and over."

I released the button and listened for a few seconds.

A beeping sound was heard before I heard the message.

"Your distress call has been received. A response boat will be to your rescue soon. Please, be patient and do not panic. Over."

I sat down and wiped the single tear that fell from my eye. I glanced at the beeping machine that hid in the jacket.

08:24:12

I gasped at the numbers shown. How could time be passing by so fast? I grabbed the rail beside me, peering beside. The harbor looked like a thin line of nothing from my sight. I saw no approaching boat of coast guards.

I could not slip the jacket off my body because of the handcuffs. I looked at the pocket knife that fell on the boat. What if I cut it out and throw the ticking bomb in the ocean? Pfft, wrong thing to do. I could end up cutting something else by accident and exploding myself. Or the bomb could explode right after I take it off me. I couldn't bring myself to believe that the reason for my death could be that. Just on me like that.

I peered over again with a desperate face. I saw a white boat far away. I wondered whether it was the one coming to my rescue or another yacht wandering about. The trawler on which Violetta went on had disappeared for a while, completely out of sight.

I hoped rescue would arrive well before my dying time. I glanced down again, and my eyes went wide. The numbers were decreasing faster than I could orally count.

02:39:57

The boat that was coming from far away would not reach in time. Even if they arrived in time, how would they handle a girl with a bomb? I leaned against the rail, waving frantically.

"Can you guys be a bit faster?" I yelled, my words falling onto empty air.

I needed to be ready for anything. I was a woman close to death. Nobody could dare to question my intelligence. Grabbing the knife, I tore the jacket's sleeves and ripped it off my shoulders and one side.

I blinked furiously and flinched as the beeping sound became louder in volume. I screeched when I saw the numbers decreasing below a minute. I stood up, with the jacket hanging onto one side. I should rip it off and thrown it into the sea urgently, but I couldn't.

A part of me was scared that it'll go off the moment I took it off.

Thirty seconds left. More tears started to fall.

Watching the numbers fall, I grabbed the edge of the jacket. It would be challenging to throw it away with both hands tied together. Heat rose from inside my shirt, making me feel weaker and sweaty.

Ten seconds left.

Let's do it!

With a shaky breath, I swung the jacket out of me and threw it over the rail. At this point, the yacht was moving forward at a moderate pace. I closed my eyes with a frown, waiting.

The next thing I knew, a jet of water hit the behind of the boat, pushing me off it and into the sea.

My head hit the surface first, making me gulp the salty water. I gasped above the water, but the sudden currents pushed my head underneath away. I flapped my legs, trying to reach the surface without my useless hands.

My lungs and every cell in my body cried for oxygen as my head started to pound. The seawater burned my eyes, and I felt my body sinking deeper instead of rising.

I felt the first rush of water entering my nose, burning its way through. The lack of oxygen increased my headache, and the black blotches that filled my vision gave me a heavy feeling. I couldn't realize whether my eyes were still open or closed. And as my body swayed around the vagueness, I realised how silent and calm drowning was.

☆☆☆

I felt myself regain consciousness with something pressing through my mouth. Was it the pressure of the water, or was I already dead?

I something else suddenly hit my chest hard enough for me to sit straight up, spitting water out of my mouth and gasping.

I squinted my eyes open a bit as my eyes were burning. I felt a hand rubbing my back as I repeatedly coughed through my burning throat. It was a human! I was saved!

"Oh God, I'm alive!" I croaked with a laugh, hugging my savior, whoever was supporting me from behind. "Yes, thanks to me," a familiar voice reverberated, and the person chuckled and patted my back.

"Ughh, who asked you to come?" I groaned as I let go slowly and coughed out a bit more water.

Castiel patted my back again, a bit more harshly this time.

"Is that a way to thank someone who dived so deep into the sea to save you? Imagine all the unconscious weight I had to pull up," he said, and I looked at his wet black hair pushed back and dripping clothes. My eyes went around the boat, from the man controlling the helm to the other stranger talking on a radio.

"What's new?" I muttered to myself and sighed.

"Get up. We've arrived," Castiel said, getting up and stretching out his hand. I looked up at him and felt too weak to lift my hand.

"Can you drag me up yourself? I haven't eaten anything for three days. I have no energy left in me- oh, wait, wait, what are you doing?" I ended as he lifted me in his arms.

"Shut up. You owe me a lot as it is," he grumbled as he walked out of the boat and onto the dock. I fell limp back in his arms with a tired, grumpy face.

"Haelyn!" I heard someone yelling.

I weakly looked up at my father running along the dock towards us.

"Let me down, quick!" I whispered to Castiel, who shrugged before letting me on my feet. My legs started acting all weird and wobbly. I grabbed his arm for support.

Dad arrived before me, his eyes darting up and down, searching. I straightened myself as best as possible and smiled, clearing my throat.

"I'm fi- omph!"

Dad's arms wrapped around me, squeezing the breath out of me. My frail arms made their way around him, reassuring him that I was fine.

"I was so worried when I didn't find you back there," he whispered with a shaky breath as he released me.

"Sorry," I mumbled, avoiding his tired eyes that were looking at me.

"You should be. Giving me such stress and tension at this old age of mine," he chuckled, jokingly slapping my shoulders. I let out a weak chuckle as well.

Dad looked over my shoulder at the awkward audience.

"Thanks for saving her, son. I knew I could always count on you."

"Anytime, sir," was the immediate reply that made me roll my eyes though the smile stayed on my face. He'd save me any time and add each time to my debt list. No, thanks.

"Haelyn! My girl! How I missed you!" an exaggerated cry grabbed my attention, as well as everyone around who turned to look for the culprit.

I laughed in embarrassment at the weird friend waving at me frantically as he ran.

"Why is his tie around his head, though?" I questioned his look.

"Is there any logic in that brain of his anyway? Let's go away," Dad said, amusedly at the clown.

"No, no. I don't want to make your abduction or your near-death situation sound as small as that, but it was only meant to pose as a distraction," Cooky explained.

"That bitch tried to kill me, and you call that distraction?" I confirmed with pursed lips and crossed arms.

We were sitting in the office two days after my freedom from the devil's grasp. I spent most of my time sleeping and eating, which I missed dearly. Dad returned home because of the mounting work due to him leaving suddenly because of me.

He remembered to appoint Castiel as the watchman in his stead to ensure any other similar mishaps did not happen again. So now, I got dragged by his side to the office, not that I would complain. Of being at the office, that is.

But I found the discussion annoying, which again returned to Cooky's argument. Violetta wanted to explode me as a distraction, it seemed. But Raphael told me to be grateful that I escaped without actually exploding to bits. I heard about the building that eventually crumbled because there was insufficient time to search each bomb she hid around.

Most of the people were successfully evacuated though some sustained injuries. Angelia was at the hospital for a night because she got a minor hit on the head. And some other people held captive at Violetta's place were still in the hospital because most of them overdosed because of her.

"So...what was exactly her plan again?" I asked, my face resting on my hands as I stared at Cooky for an explanation.

"You know that Violetta had been testing new drugs at that building, right?" Raphael asked.

"No."

"Uhm, okay. Well, she had been doing that. And most of the already tested ones were being sent in large amounts at the harbor. We got to know that from one of the workers arrested. And Violetta had the habit of frequently changing places not to attract attention. Her best plan seemed to be to destroy the building and run away, not caring if anyone got killed along the way," Raphael elaborated.

"But we put our nose in her business, which is our business too. And that was preventing her from shipping her drugs away. So she must have thought that if we focus on saving you and the others, she should slip away without any intervention," Shooky ended.

"There is usually that moment where we go, 'but that's where she thought wrong' after that," I looked at them encouragingly.

They all looked at each other and gazed at me weirdly. I slumped back in my seat as I understood.

"She hasn't been seen at any port yet, and her workers claim she may have fled among the shipments of drugs, wherever they were destined to. This could mean leaving the country. As for that Doctor, we still cannot find his real identity. We're still searching," Castiel added.

"Alessio?" I asked.

"Got him," Raphael chuckled. "He felt quite enraged at his beloved sister's betrayal and the fact that he was mistaken as just one among her workers. Must already be planning his escape and revenge."

The discussion continued until Castiel checked the time and told me to get going. I almost forgot that I was supposed to catch the night flight back home.

"Have a nice flight, both of you," Raphael winked at us.

"What does he mean, both of us?" I asked Castiel as he directed me out.

"I'm returning too if you didn't know."

"Why so early?"

"We'll all be returning anyway. So who cares when. And what if you get abducted at the airport or off the plane back in London? People love targeting you nowadays," Castiel replied sarcastically.

"Don't act like this is your main concern. I am sure many report writings are waiting for you back home. How fun!"

"Same goes for you," he dryly retorted back.

"You're in for a surprise then." "You spent so much time in Italy, and you buy me chocolate from London airport when you return? Seriously?" Eliyah eyed the chocolates in a judgmental way but grabbed them all when I tried taking them back.

"Same thing. It's all about the intention."

"Yes, but these chocolates haven't breathed Italy's air. That makes a vast difference."

"I breathed Italy's air. Want me?" I asked from my desk.

"I already got you," she winked at me, and I laughed. "That's the gift you will be giving Attorney Kim?" she chuckled at the envelope in my hands.

"Definitely, which makes me remember that I have to go straight to him now," I said, standing up.

"I know I'm telling you this for the millionth time, but let's have a sleepover for real. You always seemed to slip away. If you disappear, I don't care who I have to chase behind this time, but I will drag you back to my apartment and keep you hostage myself," Eliyah promised with a healthy smile.

"Gladly," I replied, walking away towards the elevator.

I got off the fifth floor and headed to Attorney Kim's office. I knocked on his door before entering with a greeting grin.

"Looong time, Boss," I said.

"Who are you, again?" he replied, rolling his eyes.

"Missed me that much?" I asked, taking a seat.

"You know how much work you left behind and how much you have accumulated?" he asked, his eyes glinting over his glasses.

"Is there?" I laughed as I slipped the letter into my hand.

He reached for the letter and opened it, silently reading it. He nodded, putting it back in the envelope and into his drawer.

"Good. We won't need to fire your replacement then," he mused.

I gasped with fake indignation.

"How good is she?" I demanded.

"He is quite good." "You never said that for me," I mumbled, standing up. "But, one day, I will return. And I will be stronger!"

"Close the door when you step out," Attorney Kim replied.

I gazed at him with an intense look.

"And good luck with whatever you are planning," he said. I nodded with satisfaction and walked out.

I got out of Castiel's car as he finished parking it in the parking lot at the IOF headquarters. After a week, everyone finally returned from Italy, and I thought of seeing them at the office. To pry for information, of course.

"Why are you bringing your bag as well?" Castiel asked as we marched to the meeting room.

"I want to," I said, shrugging.

Castiel surveyed me suspiciously.

"Are you curious?" I smiled, patting my bag.

"Not at all," Castiel rolled his eyes, focusing ahead.

We soon entered the meeting room, where everyone was seated and chatting.

"Heeeey, amico!" I waved around.

Raphael waved back as enthusiastically. He even dragged a seat beside him for me.

"How's life been without me for a week?" He asked with a grin.

"Just like it's been for twenty-four years before you arrived in my life," I chuckled.

"I empathize greatly. How did you even live twenty-four years without me?" he asked wonderfully.

"Trust me. She managed perfectly fine. She's already worst living with herself."

Raphael and I glared at the intruder whose seat had to, unfortunately, be beside me. Castiel shrugged and returned our glares with a smile.

"How cute," Raphael exclaimed, reaching his hand over me and towards Castiel, pinching his cheek. I slapped a hand over my mouth to stop the laugh that threatened to slip away.

"Hey, don't fight. I'm in the middle!" I tried to remind the two men as hands started being thrown in front of me.

I sighed and looked at Cooky, who stared at the two men, from across the table, in amusement.

"Psst, Cooky! Any sign of Violetta yet?"

"I am Lucio, Haelyn. Drop the nickname already. And no. She must have gone on a temporary hiding. I fear we won't hear from her soon. But I got something. Wait."

He got up and grabbed a laptop. Sitting down again, he searched for something and turned the laptop towards me.

"That's the doctor!" I exclaimed, mouth agape. "You found his identity?"

"Hans Wilhelm. German. 55 years old. He was kicked out of the country for past illegal research he did as a scientist. He used to sell data acquired from those research. Seems like he never stopped even after leaving," Cooky shrugged, taking the laptop back.

I nodded in amazement. I scrunched my nose in disgust as I thought he was twice Violetta's age. Each to their taste.

Mr Ford entered the meeting room soon after, silencing everyone's talks.

"We must go over what is to be revealed to the media. Usually, we reveal only as much as they discovered, but this time, the bombing received much public attention and even arrived on the front page of many Italian articles. The name Verdino spread like fire around. Everyone is wondering if the Verdinos have appeared again," he explained.

The discussion continued as everyone inputted what needed to be included or taken out. Shooky was responsible for writing the report and submitting it to the media.6 After their meeting ended, I waited for everybody to start going out. I took the papers from my bag and handed them to Mr. Ford.

"I'll get in touch with you soon," he smiled, and I nodded.

I turned around, leaving the room to find Castiel waiting beside the door.

"You can ask," I said, muffling my laughter.

"What makes you think I want to ask something?" he scoffed.

"You don't? Okay," I smiled in return.

We walked to the car, and as I got in, I heard the door at the back opening and someone else getting in. I turned back, thinking it was Raphael, and gasped.

"Embry!" I exclaimed, looking at the younger version of Castiel.

"Were you waiting around here?" Castiel grunted, fastening his seatbelt.

I ignored him and turned to his brother. "When did you come here?" "I'm here with my girlfriend," he grinned at me and turned to Castiel. "Cas, drop me at the library near Stallion Street."

"Are you in your second year of university right now?" I asked as Embry leaned forward between Castiel's and my seat.

"I am in the middle of the holidays right now. The second year will start soon. Oh, and I didn't expect to see you with him, you know?" he asked with gleaming eyes.

"Anything's possible," I shrugged, chuckling.

"Really? Did you finally gather your guts and profess?" Embry turned to Castiel, asking with excitement.

"Embry...you're not letting the man drive," I chuckled as I saw Castiel sitting stiff in his seat, with pursed lips and his hands grasping the steering wheel tightly. "And by the way, I learned about the love letter prank you pulled on him by using-"

The car screeched and came to a halt.

"Get out. We've arrived," Castiel breathed out as he loosened his tie.

I looked out and saw that we were in front of the library. I let out a breath of disappointment and turned to Embry.

"Let's meet up later," I smiled as he grinned and nodded, throwing a wink at Castiel.

Embry got out, making his way toward a girl. That must have been his girlfriend. Castiel started the car again, grumbling about how I had too much free time.

"I've quit my job, remember?" I reminded him with an annoying grin.

"Start searching for another job...," he trailed off in thoughts. I looked at him questioningly.

"What papers you give, Mr. Ford?" he finally asked when we stopped at the red light.1

"Finally, you asked. I filled in the papers for the training program," I grinned at him.

"You plan to join.," he drawled off, and I shook my head.

"I am only joining the training programme with Dad's encouragement. And if I can, I'll do the six months internship. Then, I'll see what I can do," I explained.

"Ain't it starting soon?"

"Yes, next week. I'm leaving for Manchester in a few days," I grimaced at the thought of leaving yet again. The conversation lapsed into silence for a while before I spoke again.

"By the way...I owe you a lot, it seems," I started, glancing at Castiel.

"You sure as hell do," he mumbled with a smirk.

"How do I repay your idiot ass then?" I smiled in turn. "Hmm, many ways.," he mused.

"You're giving me weird imaginations," I shuddered.

"If you want those im-"

"No, I don't. And where are you even driving to? We passed by your apartment like five minutes ago."

"Up to you. You have free time all day, right?" he asked nonchalantly.

I smiled, thinking about it. I turned to him, beaming. "I'll buy you lunch! One step towards repaying my debt. I need to do that soon since I'll be gone for months. What say?"

"Works for me. But I'll be glad to make it a lifetime's worth of debt for you. I saved your life after all."

And as we moved through the traffic, our back-and-forth banter made me temporarily forget what awaited me next week.

A new destination. Paved by my ambitions. With new adventures. But please, no more abductions. I had enough memories and debts to last a lifetime.

The End

OTHER BOOKS BY THE AUTHOR

Karmic Love

Undercover

Eternal Love

Undying Lust

The Good Taste

Offence and Justice

A Model for Murder

Lethal Legacy

Lethal Legacy 2

Paranormal Club

Enchanted Souls

Beginners of Nowhere

Wildflower

Mystic Agent

Dark Angel

Lonesome Moonlight

The Eerie Egg

A Romantic Crime